A Baron for All Seasons

The Brides of North Barrows #3

CLAIRE DELACROIX

Books by Claire Delacroix

Medieval Romance

The Champions of St. Euphemia
The Crusader's Bride
The Crusader's Heart
The Crusader's Kiss
The Crusader's Vow
The Crusader's Handfast

Blood Brothers
The Witch & the Wolf

The Rogues of Ravensmuir:
The Rogue
The Scoundrel
The Warrior

The Jewels of Kinfairlie:
The Beauty Bride
The Rose Red Bride
The Snow White Bride
The Ballad of Rosamunde

The True Love Brides:
The Renegade's Heart
The Highlander's Curse
The Frost Maiden's Kiss
The Warrior's Prize

The Brides of Inverfyre:
The Mercenary's Bride
The Runaway Bride

Rogues & Angels:
One Knight Enchanted
One Knight's Return

The Bride Quest:
The Princess
The Damsel
The Heiress
The Countess
The Beauty
The Temptress

REGENCY ROMANCE

The Brides of North Barrows:
Something Wicked This Way Comes
A Duke by Any Other Name
A Baron for All Seasons
A Most Inconvenient Earl

TIME TRAVEL ROMANCE

Once Upon a Kiss
The Last Highlander
The Moonstone
Love Potion #9

For information about Deborah Cooke contemporary
romances and paranormal romances, please visit:

HTTP://DEBORAHCOOKE.COM

PROLOGUE

London—January 1812

The first of us to fall prey to the parson's mousetrap!" Sebastian Montgomery crowed, saluting Alexander Armstrong as he dropped into the leather chair in the library of his Mayfair townhouse. As was customary, the earl did not spill a drop of his brandy, although it wasn't his first of the night—or morning, as it were. The liquid sloshed in the snifter but didn't slip over the edge.

"Impressive," Rupert Haskell murmured and the Earl of Rockmorton grinned.

"Practice makes perfect, my good friend," Montgomery replied.

"I would wager you had drunk London dry with your practice," Alexander, the Duke of Inverfyre, noted with a smile.

Montgomery laughed. "No, no, the feat is to feign a large consumption while imbibing comparatively little. Far better for the budget." He patted his flat belly, encased in one of his lavishly embroidered silk waistcoats. "And the fit of my wardrobe."

"Not to mention the liver," Rupert added. He chose, as had become his habit, the chair furthest from the fire and only perched on the lip of the seat, while his two friends lounged at ease in their chairs. It changed a man to have his legacy snatched away. Rupert would never take any situation for granted again.

The three had become immediate friends upon their arrival at Eton years before, and had been consistently involved in adventures together while at school. The son of an earl, the son of a duke and the son of a baron, they had oft jested of how they would change society once they were of age.

Though they were of similar height and age, each as trim and athletic as the other, their coloring and situations were different: Montgomery, a much-favored only child, always took the lead; Alexander was more considering of other views, as befit a man with a younger sister to defend; Rupert, who had been an only child but one who faced greater criticism than Montgomery, was possessed of quick wits and a quicker smile.

They remained fast friends and confidantes, though only Alexander and Montgomery had come into their inheritances. Rupert, in contrast, never would though he strove to avoid any bitterness. The financial disparity among the trio could have driven them apart: instead, they had become closer in recent years. Alexander had hired Rupert as his valet and brought him into his secret task of spying for the crown. Montgomery could be relied upon for a loan or even an outright gift, although Rupert was more likely to ask for a favor, if he had need of assistance. The trio would still do any deed for each other and Rupert was beyond glad of the friendship and support of his oldest friends.

Montgomery toasted Alexander before sipping. He winced, baring his teeth. "Liquid fire. It is good for what ails me."

"And so much ails you," Alexander teased, rolling his eyes. They laughed together.

Montgomery's library was lined with books that he did not read and always had a roaring fire as well as a full decanter of brandy. It was a comfortable haven after their night savoring the pleasures of town. On this night, they had dined and they had danced; they had visited the theater and ultimately Alexander and Montgomery had gambled, all in the name of celebrating Alexander's pending nuptials. The clock in the hall chimed two and Rupert thought of his early start the next morning. He would have laundry to do before he slept this night.

Alexander had surrendered his townhouse to his betrothed, her sister and her grandmother, while he stayed with Montgomery. Rupert had a room in the servant's quarters and knew that Montgomery's staff would notice any anomalies in his conduct of his duties. He would be up at dawn to prepare Alexander's clothes for the day, polish his boots and press his cravat.

Watson, Montgomery's butler, gave a slight tap at the door and Rupert bounded to his feet, taking a place behind Alexander's chair. Watson, an older man and a severe custodian of decency, gave Rupert a look that could have curdled a man's blood. His gaze dropped pointedly to the glass Rupert had abandoned alongside the chair he had been occupying and he inhaled sharply in disapproval. "Will there be anything else, sir?" he asked in a frosty tone, bowing to Montgomery.

Montgomery, of course, had not missed the older man's reaction. "No, Watson, unless you would care to join us." He lifted his glass again even as the butler's horror showed for the barest moment. "We are saluting the cleverness of His Grace's valet."

"Indeed." Watson surveyed Alexander's attire, as flamboyant as was customary when the duke was in town, and if anything, his disapproval grew.

There were rhinestones on the duke's cuffs and glittering down the front of his waistcoat. His breeches were striped cerise and forest green, his coat was crimson, his waistcoat was chartreuse and there was a sprig of holly in his lapel. There were even three little bells replacing the tassels on his boots that jingled as he walked. Rupert thought Alexander looked like a demented elf, but it had been his friend's scheme to act as a dandy, the better that his wits be underestimated and his presence overlooked. The guise had served him well as a spy, but Alexander meant to retire now that he was to wed. Rupert was glad his garb would change. The silks and taffetas were a fearsome amount of work to maintain.

Watson clearly was not enchanted by the duke's appearance. Judging by the tight-lipped glance he granted Rupert, he might even have laid the blame for Alexander's sartorial flair at his valet's feet.

Montgomery, in contrast, favored the severe simplicity of Beau Brummel's suggestion, with dark chausses and coat, white shirt and cravat. His only ornamentation was his collection of embroidered silk waistcoats, one in every possible hue. Alexander dressed similarly when he was not in town, and Rupert looked forward to the return of his more austere wardrobe.

"Indeed," Montgomery said again. "I see you noted the extra glass, Watson, but Haskell here has revealed and captured the jewel thief that has plagued London society for years. Is that not fiendishly clever? Does it not deserve a small reward?"

Even Watson had to acknowledge this, though he did so with only a minute nod.

Montgomery enthused. "He caught Nathaniel Cushing in the act of absconding with the Eye of India at Castle Keyvnor. And saved the damsel in distress who the duke will wed." He saluted Rupert and apparently drank, but this time Rupert noted that the level of liquid in the glass did not diminish. "How frightfully enterprising of him, don't you think, Watson?"

The older man inclined his head slightly. "Most commendable, my lord."

"All while ensuring I looked sufficiently splendid to win myself a bride," Alexander added jovially. "Our journey to Cornwall was not without incident, to be sure." Earl and duke clinked glasses and drank in tribute to their own good fortune.

"Do not neglect to mention, my lord, that your health is infinitely improved by the sea air, perhaps even sufficiently so that Dr. MacEwan will permit you the season in London," Rupert added.

"The entire season?" Montgomery echoed in delight. "We shall find trouble to be certain!"

"I shall introduce my betrothed to society," Alexander corrected with a firmness that revealed his true nature. "She has not yet enjoyed a season."

"My felicitations to you on your pending nuptials, Your Grace," Watson said with a bow.

"I thank you, Watson. I am most pleased." Alexander gestured to the bottle of brandy, his eyes filled with mischief. "Will you join us, then?"

Watson took a step back, so affronted by this breach of protocol that he nearly fled the room. "I should not be so familiar, sir, but thank you for the offer." He bowed deeply and Rupert watched Alexander and Montgomery exchange amused glances.

"Then there will be nothing else, Watson," Montgomery said. "Alexander knows his way to his chamber. I say, could there be kippers for breakfast? I like them after a night of indulgence."

"Is that not every night?" Alexander murmured, his eyes sparkling.

"As many as I can contrive," Montgomery ceded easily.

"I will ensure that there are kippers, my lord." Watson bowed again. "Good night then, my lord and Your Grace." He bowed again then took his leave, quietly closing the door behind himself. Alexander waved Rupert back to his seat as Montgomery topped up his brandy.

"Hazard pay," Montgomery teased with a wink, then settled back in his own chair. "He will be watching you like the proverbial hawk."

"He already is," Rupert agreed. "But you need not feel sorry for me. I am most comfortable." The servant's chambers in Montgomery's house did not compare with his room at either of Alexander's houses, but they were more than adequate. Rupert was glad he did not have to share the small chamber with another servant.

The fire blazed merrily and snow fell outside the windows. The three men sat companionably, legs stretched out and ankles crossed.

"A bride," Montgomery said again, shaking his head at Alexander. "I suppose it is love?"

"Of course!" Alexander said. "She has stolen my heart away forever."

Montgomery rolled his eyes at this. "But then you always believed in love and romance, a legacy from your parents." They were silent for a moment in acknowledgement of the passing of that happy pair some years before. "Haskell and I remain the skeptical ones."

"What nonsense is this?" Alexander jested. "You fall in love daily."

"Hourly," Montgomery agreed with a wise nod. "It is best. I suppose you will be tedious and wed with haste?"

"I have the special license, but Anthea wrote that she is on her way," Alexander said. Rupert couldn't keep himself from glancing up in surprise, for he was unaware of these tidings. He felt the back of his neck heat in fear that his secret admiration of the duke's sister might have been noted but no one glanced his way. "We will await her arrival."

"Miss Armstrong has such excellent taste," Montgomery said with approval. "She will put the perfect touch upon the nuptials, to be sure. It is a shame that she abandoned London so quickly in her debut season. The prospect of encountering her made any jaunt so much more interesting."

Rupert felt himself bristle at this hint of Montgomery having an interest in Miss Armstrong. She deserved far better! Montgomery was a good friend, but he treated women abominably.

"She could not do otherwise, to her thinking, not with such a pall hanging over her name," Alexander said, clearly still annoyed that his sister had been accused without cause.

"Mr. Nathaniel Cushing has much to answer for," Rupert said with conviction.

Alexander regarded him. "And I suspect he paid some of that debt when he was caught for this most recent crime."

"It was only right," Rupert agreed. "It was cowardly to allow innocent young women to take the blame for his thefts."

"Or one particular innocent young woman?" Montgomery mused, as perceptive as ever.

"It was wrong. He was wrong." Rupert could not subdue the heat in his tone. "And I for one am glad that he is now facing the consequences of his actions."

They drank again, united in their agreement.

"But what of the gems?" Montgomery asked. "Were all his spoils recovered and returned to their original owners?"

"No, and that is the rub," Alexander said. "He had nothing in his possession. I wager they were all sold promptly and have now been scattered."

Rupert could not keep silent. "They must be found, though. Is there no scheme to do as much?"

Alexander considered him. "I have not been requested to do as much."

"Of course, there would have been insurance paid," Montgomery noted.

Alexander nodded agreement.

Rupert could not leave the matter alone. "But your sister..."

Both friends watched him silently. Rupert fell silent, thinking he had said too much.

"My sister," Alexander invited finally.

Rupert frowned. "Surely she will be suspected of having the gem until it is revealed to be elsewhere, or until it is returned. The stain upon her reputation will linger and she may find that many will spurn her company."

Alexander scowled at this prospect.

"He is right," Montgomery concurred. "They will whisper when she enters any room. You know how they are. Veritable vultures when it comes to reputation and gossip."

"I realize as much, but what is to be done?" Alexander said. "It has been ten years. The gem could be anywhere!"

"I would find it," Rupert said. "Or try to do as much, for Miss Armstrong's sake."

His old friends exchanged a glance and Rupert feared neither of them were in doubt as to his feelings. Not that he could act upon them, not when he was a mere valet. He could not regret his words to his father but he could regret their result.

"What a wretched moment for a man to be without a legacy," Montgomery drawled, his eyes glinting as he watched Rupert. "You could reconcile with the old man, you know."

Rupert shook his head. "So long as he disgraces my mother by flaunting his affair with Mrs. Blythe, I cannot speak to him with civility."

"How many brats has she borne him?"

"One boy."

"Is that not a foul situation?" Montgomery said, clearly not caring a whit. "I would contrive for all my friends to be rich, no matter the cost to others."

"There is nothing to be done for it." Rupert drained his glass. He was more fortunate than he might have been and he knew it. That was also thanks to Alexander, and he would not dishonor that man's name or sister at any price.

He would clear her reputation, even if he could do no more than that.

"Indeed," Alexander noted. "I am glad to have been able to share some advantage with you."

"And I am grateful, Your Grace. As you well know."

Alexander winced. "You need not address me thus when we are alone."

"But one can never be certain that we *are* alone."

"Truly, if Watson were not so principled, he might be listening at the door," Montgomery said. "He was so disappointed when my father died and the title fell into my undeserving grasp. Although I confess it is good fun to startle him."

"You should wed and redeem yourself in the eyes of your staff," Alexander suggested.

Montgomery laughed. "Not I!" He gestured with his glass. "It will have to be Rupert who succumbs next."

"There is little chance of that," Rupert replied evenly. "Even though my wages are generous for my station, my purse is not sufficiently fat to tempt a lady."

"And you will not wed beneath your station," Alexander said with approval.

"Take a mistress," Montgomery suggested. "Or two."

"He cannot afford two," Alexander noted.

"Just one will improve your mood, Haskell," Montgomery insisted. "I can suggest several candidates."

"I will guess that you will decline to suggest one in particular," Rupert teased, for he had heard the gossip.

Montgomery laughed. "I will not share Miss Ballantyne any more than is necessary, to be sure. Keep your maiden, Alexander, and enjoy her. I favor a woman who knows what she is about in the bedroom." He swirled the brandy in his glass and sighed with satisfaction. "Ah, Esmeralda."

Alexander ignored this. He regarded Rupert over the lip of his own snifter. "Have you a plan for finding the gem? I will do whatever necessary to assist."

Of course, he was as concerned with Miss Armstrong's happiness as Rupert. "You should not be directly involved, for if it is found, it will simply be assumed that you surrendered what was in your possession all along." Alexander nodded at the wisdom of this, though it was clear he did not like it. "I had thought that Mr. Timothy Cushing might have a notion or two. After all, he is a collector of gems. He might know how they might be illicitly sold or where such a feat could be done."

"And he did aid us with the capture of his nephew," Alexander said. "It might be possible to contrive matters so that it looks as if he has seen the gems found and even your role could be disguised."

"Indeed."

"Shall I write to him and request that he meet with you in private?"

"That would be most helpful, Your Grace."

"Then consider it done. I should have known that you would plan for the details and ensure that all is set to rights. You are the perfect man of principle, Rupert." Before Rupert could reply, Alexander drained his glass and rose to his feet. "And now I am for bed, Montgomery. I thank you again for your hospitality."

"Do not eat all of the kippers, I beg of you," Montgomery said with a smile. "I may linger abed in the morning."

"And miss my tangerine trousers? For shame, Montgomery. They are a sight to behold, but will leave my wardrobe soon," Alexander said.

"Mercifully," Rupert murmured and the three of them laughed together again.

Montgomery waved a hand. "Be sure to discard this particular ensemble, too. It is distinctive, to be sure, but utterly hideous."

Alexander bowed as if accepting a compliment and they laughed again before parting for the night.

At least he had convinced Alexander of the importance of finding that gem. Rupert would resolve the matter in Miss Armstrong's favor and be content with rendering that service to the lady who held his heart.

It was not enough to satisfy, but he would have to be content.

No doubt it would become easier in time.

CHAPTER ONE

Anthea Armstrong was never fond of travelling, but this journey had been a plague upon her patience from start to finish. The roads were often challenging in the winter, but the heavy rains in the north of England this year had turned many of them to mire. They had poor luck with inns and had seldom been able to book the better rooms—one fateful night in York, they had not found a room at all. This had occurred even though Findlay had abandoned Airdfinnan to guarantee her safe passage to London, and Anthea was convinced her brother's butler was better than most at seeing matters resolved with satisfaction. The weather had been miserable, her maid Connaught had come down with a cold, and the combination had left Anthea exhausted.

On the one hand, she had never been so glad to

arrive in London in her life. She might fall at her brother Alexander's feet and weep with gratitude when they reached his townhouse in Mayfair. Perhaps the Fates recognized her reluctance to even go to town and contrived to make her appreciate the opportunity.

On the other hand, Anthea had plenty of time to question the wisdom of her decision to leave Airdfinnan during their arduous journey. Her brother's Scottish house had become her refuge and sanctuary these past years, and it only made sense that abandoning it left her with doubts.

Never mind that she would see again many of those who had witnessed her mortification in her debut season. To be accused of theft was a horror she would never forget, even though her innocence had finally been proven and the true culprit apprehended. She would be able to hold up her head in society again and that was one reason she had chosen to come south.

The greater reason was the chance that her elusive suitor of her debut season might take up his courtship again. Did she dare to hope that he was yet unwed? That he might remember her? The very notion made her shiver with anticipation.

To wed for love would be perfect bliss, in Anthea's opinion, and she was glad her older brother had found such joy. Of course, she wanted to meet Miss Daphne Goodenham, the lady in question, and her younger sister, Eurydice, and even their opinionated grandmother, Lady North

Barrows. Anthea already had received a number of letters from Miss Goodenham and was convinced they would like each other. She seemed to be both cheerful and sensible, a very happy combination.

Not to mention the vine. A seed of the legendary vine of Airdfinnan had sprouted during Alexander's courtship of Daphne, just as the tale had insisted it would for the heir of their family holding. Anthea—who had insisted Alexander take a seed with him—wanted to see the plant. Surely, it could not be as vigorous as all insisted.

But the greater concern was the fate of her most alluring partner. Anthea stared out the window, not really seeing the crowded road, and remembered an evening as dark and mysterious as this winter morning was bright.

The masquerade ball.

Maman loved a masquerade ball and invariably hosted one to launch the season when she was in town. That this one would also mark the beginning of her only daughter's debut season meant that it had to be more spectacular than usual. Papa had granted permission to do whatsoever was desired, and Anthea had been thrilled.

On the night in question, the townhouse might have been turned into a fairy palace. The rooms glittered with decorations, tiny candles and sparkling arrangements of flowers. Great sweeps of white embroidered cloth hung from the walls, making the ballroom look like a massive tent, filled with shadows and innuendo. The night was uncommonly warm for the time of year, so the doors to the courtyard were open and a breeze wafted through the ballroom, carrying the sound of laughter over the music. The combination was magical.

Anthea felt particularly splendid herself, in a new silk dress of emerald green, embroidered with gold on the hems. She had been loaned a parure from her mother's collection for the night, an elegant concoction of faceted citrines set in gold. She had gold slippers and a gossamer ivory shawl—and butterflies in her stomach when she descended the stairs. Guests were already arriving and Findlay announced them at the door in his most sonorous voice. The street was crowded with carriages, guests lined the steps to the street, and the hall already filled with women in their glittering splendor.

The orchestra played and the champagne flowed, Papa laughed with pride as he escorted her and Maman into the ballroom, one on each arm—and Alexander could not be discerned from the bevy of masked men awaiting the opportunity to dance with her. Anthea couldn't have been more excited. Papa and Maman led the first dance, then Papa escorted Anthea to the dance floor. She could only conclude that the masked man who danced with her mother was Alexander, and indeed, she recognized his signature grace.

She was breathless from dancing with Alexander when she felt someone behind her. Alexander smiled and bowed, and Anthea pivoted as the man bowed low. He was taller than her with dark brown wavy hair and his eyes seemed to sparkle behind his black domino mask. His lips were firm, and he smiled slightly as she met his gaze. There was an intensity about his manner that made Anthea catch her breath. He was a little more slender than her brother and

Anthea's heart skipped a beat at the weight of his survey. She had no notion of his identity, which made his interest all the more exciting. Alexander had vanished into the throng, leaving no one to make introductions.

"Will you dance with a mysterious stranger?" the stranger asked, his voice a low rumble. He raised a brow. "Even without the benefit of an introduction?

"Do you not mean to confess your name, sir?"

"Then I would be neither mysterious nor a stranger, and it is my understanding that both have an allure for lovely young ladies like yourself."

Anthea felt her cheeks heat. "I thank you, sir, for the compliment."

"It is only the truth, Miss Armstrong. You are the most beauteous woman in the room, and the veritable queen of the ball. It is that and only that which prompts me to boldly present myself, without any soul to vouch for my character."

"I hope your character is above repute, sir. I would hesitate to dance with any man whose companionship might sully my reputation."

"I grant you my solemn word, Miss Armstrong, that I have no desire to put a shadow upon your name, and indeed, I would defend it and you with my dying breath."

"You seem most devoted for a stranger, sir."

"Perhaps your beauty strikes me to the heart." He smiled. "Or perhaps we are not so unknown to each other as you might assume." His gaze was warm and Anthea's mouth went dry. He bowed and offered his gloved hand.

Though she knew she should wait for Maman, Anthea placed her hand upon his. His fingers closed over hers, both strong and gentle, and she allowed herself to be led to the dance floor, heart racing. She caught a glimpse of her mother's smile of approval and knew his identity was not hidden from all. They must have been introduced.

He was an exquisite dancer, elegant and decisive, and he ensured that she always was turned to advantage. Soon they had a small appreciative audience, and Anthea could not resist his invitation to dance the next—and the next. By the end of the fourth dance, she was well aware that her aunt Penelope was watching them avidly.

"There are ices in the courtyard, I am given to understand," he said and Anthea would have followed him anywhere. He escorted her to the courtyard and the cool air was a sweet relief. She fanned herself as he got an ice for her and the allamande began. People moved inside to join the dance: suddenly and unexpectedly, they were quite alone in the courtyard. The night was clear and the stars shone overhead; the music and laugher carried to Anthea's ears but she felt that she enjoyed a forbidden moment with her mysterious stranger.

"I should go," she whispered.

"Will you not stay?"

Anthea could not resist. "I might if you confessed your name, sir."

"By the sparkle of your eyes, Miss Armstrong, the enigma is in my favor, and I would not lose an increment of your attention at any price." He smiled, and she thought that what she could see of his face was most handsome.

She laughed. "You tease me, sir."

He sobered. "Not in the least. Not for a moment." He leaned closer, his words low and his breath soft against her cheek. "I came this night solely in the hope of dancing with *you and now I shall depart, content."*

"You cannot leave, not so early as this."

"And yet I must, lest I be tempted to hope for more." His gaze swept down, she could see as much even through his mask, and she found herself unable to take a breath. "You are exquisite, Miss Armstrong, and a beauty to your very marrow. I wish you a most enjoyable evening."

"Will I not see you again, sir?"

"You might, at one event or another, if I can contrive it."

"Do you wish to contrive it?" she asked boldly and his smile flashed.

"More than life itself, my lady." His gaze was hot then and she felt warm all over again, but shivery as well.

"I would have a kiss to keep the memory alive," she said on impulse, startled by her own audacity.

"Miss Armstrong, you astonish me." He moved closer, though, and looked down at her, the heat of his proximity making her tingle. "But I cannot resist such temptation," he whispered, then bent to brush his lips across her cheek. In the last moment, Anthea turned her head and their lips touched with a most tantalizing heat.

It was a gentle kiss yet as different from those kisses she had known with family as might be possible. The very touch of his mouth against hers set her skin afire and made her yearn for so much more. Anthea heard the rumble of his laugh before he backed away. He surveyed her for a moment from the doorway, then bowed, spinning on his heel to stride into the ballroom. He vanished in the crowd more quickly than she might have believed possible. Though she might have pursued him in the hope of seeing his carriage or having a glimpse of some detail that would cast light upon his identity,

Anthea could not.

For her aunt caught her elbow in one hand, her grip so sure that Anthea knew her absence had been noted. She was turned to meet another gentleman, and curtsied as her aunt introduced him. The son of a marquess, but not a man she knew. "My niece and god-daughter," Aunt Penelope said to the man in question, as if to warn him, and he nodded before asking Anthea to dance.

She did not know how many partners she had or how many dances she enjoyed. Anthea could think only of one. Her lips tingled still when she finally retired and she knew she would never forget her earlier partner—or her first kiss.

When would she see him again?

There had been cards left for Anthea in the ensuing weeks, their timing almost always coinciding with her being away from the house. They had only a domino mask drawn upon them in black ink and no name, but it thrilled her each time she knew he had called. It was a tease and a reminder, a seductive game that she wanted to play to its finish. Findlay had refused to surrender any details about her caller and Anthea had looked for him at every event.

If she had encountered him again that season, she did not know of it.

Had the accusation that she was a thief eliminated his regard for her? Had he wed another since her departure? Was she a fool to hope to encounter him again?

If only she knew his name...

The carriage reached the house just before noon and the horses stamped with impatience when bidden to halt. Anthea and her party had stayed just north of London the night before and the four bays would have been content to run yet further on this day, the first sunny one of their journey. Connaught sneezed mightily as the door was swept open, revealing Alexander's London house, so white as to be radiant in the sunshine.

"Thank goodness we are finally arrived, Findlay," Anthea said, offering her hand to the butler of Airdfinnan. "Though little could have been contrived better, thanks to your efforts—" She fell silent when her gloved hand was taken by a man other than Findlay.

It was Haskell, her brother's valet.

Well, he had once been Alexander's comrade, but some misfortune had befallen him and Alexander had offered him a post. It had been most thoughtful of her brother, but Anthea had avoided Haskell. They had met years before, when she had been only ten years of age and he had come to visit Airdfinnan. She remembered those happy weeks well, and recalled her infatuation with her brother's friend with some embarrassment. He had been kind then but surely it had only been good manners at root.

Not an unbridled affection as her own had been. For years, she had told herself that it was of no import, but each time their paths crossed, her heart thundered.

As it did now. Anthea could not resist the opportunity to take a closer look. Haskell was infinitely more handsome than she had noticed previously, and his slow smile of appreciation launched a flutter in her belly. Was his mouth the same shape as that of her mysterious suitor? She could almost believe it, but reminded herself of the years that had passed.

She was being a sentimental fool.

Anthea smiled politely, even as she found herself keenly aware of the strength of the hand that braced her own.

Why had Haskell met her coach? She would find meaning even in that, so foolish was her heart. For all she knew, he loved another. Why would he not?

Once she stood on the gravel, Anthea realized she had to look up to meet Haskell's gaze. He was dangerously attractive, to be sure, and a woman could forget herself when confronted with that knowing smile and the appreciative gleam in those eyes—but he was merely a valet. Anthea was not a snob, but even this scrutiny was unsuitable.

An attraction would be more so.

That, alas, did not keep her from feeling one. She had been without male companionship too long, to be sure.

Meanwhile, Haskell bowed before her. His jacket, she could not fail to notice, fit his broad shoulders admirably, and his gaze was steady. His eyes were brown and twinkled in a most beguiling way. And his hair. Dark brown and wavy, so thick she might have been tempted to push her fingers through it.

She recalled another man with such hair then caught herself. It must be a common hue.

She was losing her wits, to be sure.

"Welcome to London, Miss Armstrong." His voice was deep. "I trust your journey was satisfactory."

"If slightly too long, Haskell," she acknowledged then averted her gaze, seeking a reason for his presence. She immediately spotted Alexander's larger coach.

"The duke is just arriving for luncheon and bade me hasten to open your door," Haskell provided.

"And I thank you for your kindness," Anthea said, shivering slightly as she spoke. The wind was cold, the sky a crisp blue overhead and a bit of frost crunching underfoot. Although the coach had seemed chilly, she now missed the warm brick that had been under her feet.

Her brother's team of six black horses nickered and shook their manes as they stood before the larger coach, such a splendid team that more than one passerby paused to admire them. It was the black coach with his emblem on the doors in gold, and every inch of it gleamed in the sunlight.

Rodney was calling from his perch atop the smaller coach to the other driver about the welfare of the horses, Findlay was directing the removal of the trunks, and Pierce, the butler now in charge of the London house, had already opened the front door. The servants were on the steps to welcome her and Anthea looked between the two butlers, wondering whether they could survive together beneath a single roof. She steeled herself to negotiate the complications of staff.

She would do it early, before matters could escalate beyond redemption.

"Cheerio, Anthea," Alexander called, raising a hand as he emerged from the larger coach and strolled toward her. His voice was higher than usual and his tone so affected that she thought for a moment it could not be her older brother at all. "How was your journey, my dear?"

Anthea blinked and stared. Her brother, rather than attired in his customary black and white, was resplendent in mauve and yellow. Every inch of his waistcoat was embroidered and his cuffs were even jeweled. She had never seen striped breeches of such vivid hues upon him before, nor so many sparkling buttons upon his garb. He carried a walking stick that flashed in the light and she was certain there had to be rouge on his cheeks. He even had developed a round belly, which she knew would have taken considerable effort to gain since they last had seen each other a month before.

But Alexander was not a glutton. He was athletic and moderate in his appetites, as well as conservative in his dress. What on earth was amiss?

He halted beside her, eyes sparkling with mischief and bowed, then surveyed her through a quizzing glass which she had never seen him use before. "Has the journey been so traumatic that you are lost for words, dear sister?"

It was a jest of some kind. It had to be. She risked a sidelong glance to discover that Haskell was utterly serious. His eyes, though, twinkled merrily. Anthea could not imagine how he could fail to be privy to Alexander's scheme, whatever it might be, and assumed he was part of it.

"Alexander," she said, unable to curb her affection even given his odd appearance, and kissed his cheek. "Whatever is wrong with you?" she whispered for his ears alone.

Alexander winked. "Naught at all, my dear sister. You see before you a happy man indeed."

Was this the influence of his intended? If so, Anthea would have words for that young woman and her horrific taste. She was more than prepared to wage war on her brother's behalf, and saw Haskell quickly swallow a smile, as if he read her thoughts. A look like quicksilver darted between the two men and she knew then that they *were* co-conspirators.

"Tell me," she insisted, but Alexander simply took her arm, guiding her toward the house.

"It is so utterly perfect that you have encountered Haskell this morning, for I know you will wish to thank him yourself," he said, his words mystifying Anthea.

She looked toward Haskell, who walked on her other side but slightly behind her. She had the sense that the pair of them were protecting her, but that was nonsense.

"I do not understand," she confessed.

"Did I not tell you that it was Haskell who so boldly revealed and captured the fiend who had besmirched your name?"

Anthea looked at Haskell, who bowed. That hair invited her touch. When he straightened, his eyes glowed so warmly that she felt herself flush as she looked away.

He was a *valet*.

"He did?"

"Indeed. Little did I know that Haskell was a spy in the service of the crown, committed to capturing the jewel thief who has plagued society these past years." Alexander tapped on Anthea's hand. "He outed the scoundrel in Bocka Morrow, no less, tackled him in the maze of Castle Keyvnor and brought him to justice. It was most impressive, even if I did have to tie my own cravat for dinner."

Haskell was a spy and the man responsible for clearing her name? A wave of gratitude swept through Anthea, one that only grew warmer when she found that man watching her.

"I grant you my solemn word, Miss Armstrong, that I have no desire to put a shadow upon your name, and indeed, I would defend it and you with my dying breath."

She remembered those whispered words with sudden clarity and the vigor with which they had been uttered.

It could not be.

Could it?

Haskell had been Alexander's friend at Eton and later at Oxford. He had come to Airdfinnan one summer. He had spent time with her instead of hunting with the others and she had thought him kind.

Perhaps there had been more to it than that.

Anthea kept her gaze locked upon Alexander. "You wrote that the thief was Nathaniel Cushing." She dared not look at Haskell again lest her thoughts be guessed.

"Indeed, he had a routine of stealing the gems he delivered as gifts for his uncle, Mr. Timothy Cushing, the famed collector." Alexander said. "He then hid the stolen gems in the luggage of innocent young ladies and robbed them after they had left the party. Haskell deduced it all!"

Anthea took a deep breath and risked another sidelong glance. Of course, Haskell's gaze was locked upon her with no small measure of admiration. She felt her cheeks heat. "He always did have a talent for seeing a quandary resolved," she said, noting his smile. "I seem to remember a clock you repaired at Airdfinnan one summer."

"Indeed, and still it keeps perfect time," Alexander said.

"I thank you for your efforts, Haskell," she said. "It is a great relief to have my name cleared and the truth known."

"But the credit is not entirely mine," Haskell said, that smile curving his mouth again so that she longed to stretch out a fingertip... "It was your tale of meeting Nathaniel Cushing after your departure from town that fixed my suspicions upon him, my lady." He bowed again. "I must thank *you* for your aid."

Anthea felt uncommonly flustered. She could not form an attachment with her brother's valet, no matter what his past fortunes had been. "So long as justice is served and all ends well."

Haskell inclined his head slightly. "Indeed. You were always possessed of good sense, Miss Armstrong."

"I cannot wait for you to meet Miss Goodenham," Alexander said, leading Anthea up the stairs. Maids curtseyed on one side and liveried footmen bowed on the other. She smiled at each one, halfway thinking that Alexander had too much staff.

"I yearn to meet her myself," she said.

"I would also ask you, Anthea, if you would not mind managing the house with your customary efficiency for the moment," he continued in a lower voice. "It would be most useful for Miss Goodenham to have a tutor in this matter and you will be the best. She has a facility with accounts, from my understanding, but there is always more to learn. You know this household, its traditions and its staff better than anyone, after all."

"Not better than you?"

He grinned. "Perhaps not."

How curious that his betrothed, who Anthea knew to be young, would have such a talent with figures. Perhaps the grandmother exaggerated her skills, though why she would choose that one to share was an enigma. Most matrons would brag of dancing skills, drawing ability or a facility with languages. Anthea wished even more to meet the ladies in question.

"It would be my pleasure," she said, aware that her brother awaited her reply. Anthea noted Pierce looking daggers at Findlay and knew precisely how she would begin.

"Ah, look, Haskell!" Alexander pounced upon a letter on the silver tray held by the first footman. "Here, no doubt, is the introduction you requested." He opened the envelope and read the missive, then handed it to Haskell, to Anthea's surprise. "Mr. Cushing will see you tomorrow at three."

"Mr. Cushing?" Anthea echoed in confusion. "I thought he had been apprehended."

Haskell cleared his throat. "Mr. *Timothy* Cushing is the gentleman I would meet and His Grace has been kind enough to arrange the matter."

"But why?"

"Not all of the stolen gems have been retrieved, my lady, and I would request an inventory from him, with descriptions, in the hope that can be achieved."

"The crown should pay your wages, Haskell," Alexander said cheerfully. "When you are always about state business instead of mine own." He smiled at Anthea. "Although I suppose there is merit in seeing a task thoroughly done."

"I should think so," Anthea agreed, curious to know more. She remembered that much-younger Haskell being teased by her brother for being good to his word, and thorough.

The man in question bowed. "With your leave, Your Grace, I will collect your new waistcoat and trousers from the tailor on the same journey."

"An excellent scheme, Haskell. I shall wear them at dinner tomorrow evening, simply to please Miss Goodenham."

Anthea dreaded the sight of them, at that endorsement. Would they be more garish than this ensemble?

"Of course, Your Grace." Haskell bowed and pivoted to leave, striding away with purpose. Anthea could not entirely curb her desire to watch.

Haskell, a spy. That did make him intriguing.

Alexander tapped a finger on her arm, drawing her attention. "I have arranged a small dinner party tomorrow night, for fear you might be too tired tonight. Aunt Penelope, of course, desires to see you, and you know Montgomery."

"It will be a delight to see Aunt Penelope and the Earl of Thornedyke." She smiled then, noticing the pair of young women who awaited them with obvious nervousness.

One woman stood in the doorway to the library, her dark gold hair, solemn manner and slightly stocky figure revealing her identity to Anthea as readily as the book clutched in her hand. This had to be the younger sister, Eurydice, and clearly she had discovered the wonders of Alexander's library. Before her and at the bottom of the stairs stood a blond maiden so lovely that Anthea blinked in awe. It did not hurt her first impression of her brother's betrothed that Miss Daphne Goodenham gazed at Alexander with adoration.

"Your Grace!" she said, her eyes shining with pleasure as she curtsied and kissed his hand. "I have missed you, sir." She was a rare beauty, to be sure. Her hair was as golden as sunlight and her eyes clear green, her lashes thick and her lips ruddy. She was slender yet feminine and so clearly besotted with Alexander that Anthea would have forgiven her anything. Indeed, she gave an impression of being very sweet and entirely genuine, which Anthea guessed would appeal mightily to her brother. He had been the target of many an ambitious mama's scheme and disliked any contrivance.

Which did nothing to explain his current mode of dress.

How she itched to know the fullness of this tale!

"And I have missed you," Alexander rumbled in his usual deep tones, bending to kiss the hand of his betrothed. "But I had an errand at the tailor, one of which you will approve, my dear, I am certain.

She smiled. "I know I shall, sir." She bestowed a warm smile upon Anthea. "And this surely is your sister, sir."

"It most certainly is." Alexander introduced them.

"I am so glad you have arrived, Miss

Armstrong," Miss Goodenham said. "Everything must be perfect for His Grace and I would request your assistance in ensuring that I make every detail as it should be."

"I understand you already influence his wardrobe."

Miss Goodenham smiled at Alexander. "The fashion is becoming so much simpler for men, and I think it would favor him well to be in black and white." She laughed a little and gestured toward his stomach with her fingertips. "And a little less pudding."

"Whatever you desire, my dear." Alexander kissed her hand again and she flushed prettily.

Anthea found herself warming to his fiancé, since she would return Alexander to the appearance Anthea knew best.

Alexander introduced the younger sister who gave a low curtsey. Her manners were exemplary but Anthea guessed that she wished to return to her book.

"What are you reading?"

"It is a novel recommended by the duke," Miss Eurydice said. "For it is about two sisters who are utterly different from each other." She turned the book, revealing it to be *Sense & Sensibility*.

"And do you like it?"

"Very much." She obviously wanted to open it and begin reading again.

"Alexander has rather good instincts when it comes to books. I cherish the ones he has given me.”

“Oh, this one is from His Grace’s library,” Miss Eurydice confessed solemnly. “It is not my book. I am simply fortunate enough to be able to read it.”

“I believe you might have time enough to finish a chapter before we dine,” Alexander said to her and the younger girl’s eyes lit. She excused herself, curtseyed again and retreated to the library with haste. “She has a fondness for the same window seat you always favored,” he said to Anthea and she smiled, feeling that she had found a kindred spirit.

“We will have to talk about books. Perhaps I will read that one when she has finished it.” Anthea smiled at Miss Goodenham. “Even though I have no sister, I have always wanted one.”

She laughed with pleasure. “And now you are to have two. Better yet, Eurydice and I will have an older sister to rely upon for advice. I understand that your taste is exquisite, Miss Armstrong. I should most appreciate your assistance in every matter. His Grace’s home is much larger than any I have lived in before, and I fear to make an error.”

“You will not,” Alexander said gallantly and she beamed at him.

“You should be a stricter critic, sir!”

“But I see nothing to criticize.”

“Of course, I will be glad to be of assistance,” Anthea said. “Alexander indicates that you wish to learn how to run his household.”

“Of course!” The younger woman flushed slightly. “I would have you call me Daphne, if it pleases you."

Anthea smiled. "And you will call me Anthea, please."

"Thank you."

"Once I see Connaught settled, we will begin." Anthea glanced back at the two butlers and lowered her voice. "We must avert disaster first."

"Oh!" Daphne said, her eyes wide. "I had not thought of that," she murmured, her worried gaze following Anthea's glance.

"It will be readily resolved and best done quickly," Anthea assured her.

"I should like to watch," the younger woman said solemnly. "If it would not trouble you."

Anthea was only too glad to have such an enthusiastic pupil. With Daphne confident in her abilities, there would be nothing binding Anthea to her brother's household.

Did she dare to hope for one of her own?

CHAPTER TWO

Haskell was checking the duke's linen when the staff belowstairs abruptly fell silent and rose to their feet. He turned to find Miss Armstrong entering the kitchen. The sight of her filled his heart with joy, just as it had the first time he had met her. If anything, she was more lovely than he recalled, tall and slender with a crown of red-gold curly hair. He had seen her only weeks before, but hourly could not be sufficient for Haskell. The young girl he had first admired had grown into a woman, still practical but infinitely more lovely.

She moved with grace and purpose into the kitchen. "Good day, everyone," she said. "Please do be seated again." Her smile put the staff immediately at ease. Not all were as quick to sit as she suggested, though: Pierce and Findlay remained standing as did the plump—and excellent—cook, Mrs. Stewart.

Even though Miss Armstrong had not been in residence at the London house for years, it was clear that she was remembered and with fondness. Once, Findlay had been the sole butler, but he had retreated to Airdfinnan to ensure her comfort and Pierce had been hired for the London house since Alexander had been spending more time in London.

Miss Goodenham followed Miss Armstrong, clearly intent upon learning her task. Haskell admired the determination of Alexander's betrothed to be the best wife possible, but he particularly savored the opportunity to openly look upon Miss Armstrong.

"Pierce and Findlay," she began and they both bowed. "I should like to immediately address the question of authority in this house while you are both in residence."

Pierce frowned slightly and Haskell guessed that he feared he would have to answer to Findlay, who had served the family much longer.

"If I may be so bold, Miss Armstrong," Findlay said with a slight bow of his head. "I should like to request a short break from service while in London. I will be glad to return to Airdfinnan whenever it suits your convenience, of course."

Miss Armstrong smiled and it seemed to Haskell that the room basked in the sight. He certainly did. "Would you tour the sights, Findlay?"

"No, I would seek some tidings of a cousin of

mine."

"Is she in town?"

"I do not know. She entered the service of a family more than twenty years ago and travelled to the West Indies with them as a governess. I have heard nothing from her in years—of course, she was inclined to correspond with my wife, gone these eight years—so I would like to see if I can learn any tidings of her while in town." Some of the newer servants gaped at Findlay for this long-winded confession, but Haskell knew the older man was given more leave to be familiar with the family.

To Rupert's surprise, Miss Goodenham's eyes widened in surprise. He knew that Miss Armstrong could not see the younger lady's reaction and wondered at its cause.

Miss Armstrong smiled at the butler. "I have no objection to such a quest, Findlay. Indeed, she may be most glad to hear from you. I hope you find her well."

The older butler inclined his head to Pierce. "Of course, I should be honored to be of any assistance in this household while I am here."

"I have all in hand..." Pierce began with his customary confidence.

"But there may be additional errands with the arrangements for the wedding," Miss Armstrong noted. "Your assistance would be invaluable in that matter, Findlay, and I shall rely upon you, rather than interrupting Mr. Pierce's routine. The house is full and there are many details to manage as it is. Of course, you must seek out your cousin, as well, but perhaps you might check with me each morning that we can best plan our forays."

"That would be ideal, Miss Armstrong," Findlay said with a bow. "I thank you kindly for the suggestion."

Haskell could not help but admire how neatly she had divided the managerial task between the two men.

"And then there will be no doubt of your wage," Miss Armstrong said.

"I thank you for your consideration, Miss Armstrong." Findlay bowed to her again.

"I think this arrangement is most admirable, Miss Armstrong," Pierce agreed. "As sensible as your reputation."

"Then we are agreed," Miss Armstrong said, bestowing a smile upon the other servants. Rupert did not know whether her gaze truly lingered upon him or whether he simply wished it to be so. "I shall not interrupt your labor any further. If we could review the menus for the week after luncheon, Pierce, I should be most grateful. I understand we are to have guests tomorrow evening and my aunt is particularly fond of Mrs. Stewart's white fish in cream sauce."

Mrs. Stewart beamed at this praise.

"Of course, Miss Armstrong," Pierce said.

"Perhaps it is not too early for fresh asparagus?" Miss Armstrong asked the cook.

"I shall be sure to seek some out, Miss

Armstrong," Mrs. Stewart said then recalled herself. "But only if it is fresh and the price is right."

"You are always so accommodating, Mrs. Stewart. I cannot imagine what my brother would do without you."

"Thank you, my lady." Mrs. Stewart curtseyed deeply.

"Miss Goodenham has professed an interest in learning all I know of managing a household, and I wonder if we might refer to some of your records, Mrs. Stewart. The volume for my debut season would be particularly helpful in planning for the season ahead. We will have dinners and breakfasts to plan."

"Of course, my lady, but prices have increased something fearful."

"Naturally, Mrs. Stewart, but it will give us a place to begin."

The cook bowed again and went to a cupboard. Within it were bound volumes of different colors, some quite worn. She handed one to Miss Armstrong, her reluctance to surrender it clearly at war with her desire to help.

"I shall ensure it is returned with haste, just as it is now," Miss Armstrong said with a reassuring smile. "Miss Goodenham can copy what she finds necessary to study."

"Very good, my lady."

Miss Armstrong turned briskly to leave but halted when Miss Goodenham, still behind her, did not more. "Excuse me, Findlay," the younger lady said and all gazes rose to her. "What was the name of your cousin?"

The butler raised a brow. "I should not trouble you with it, Miss Goodenham."

"But I believe a friend of mine had a governess named Miss Findlay."

Rupert wondered at this, for it seemed from her manner that the lady told a small falsehood. To what purpose?

"Miss Amelia Findlay was her name," Findlay supplied with pride.

Color suffused the cheeks of the duke's betrothed. "Oh, then I am mistaken. My friend's governess had the given name, Harriet. I apologize for even mentioning as much."

"I am most obliged by your desire to assist, Miss Goodenham," the butler said with a bow.

The two women left then, the younger glancing back with some trepidation. Rupert saw Miss Armstrong's hand fall to Daphne's elbow, urging her back upstairs, and knew he had not been the only one to notice her reaction.

The kitchen erupted in chatter then, the two butlers shaking hands with each other over their new division of duties. The housekeeper commanded one of the footmen to show Findlay to his room and Mrs. Stewart ordered a girl to make haste in peeling vegetables for dinner. Rupert bent his attention upon that cravat again and tried to compile a list of questions for his appointment with Mr. Timothy Cushing.

It was a wiser use of his time than recalling the beauty of Miss Armstrong's smile.

Though indeed, the curve of those lips made him recall his first glimpse of her...

Rupert had always known that Alexander Armstrong had a sister, of course, and that the siblings were fond of each other. That had not prepared him for his first glimpse of her—or his reaction to meeting her. He had never believed in love, let alone love at first sight, not until Anthea Armstrong.

Rupert's father had even left his mistress in London in order to accept an invitation from the Duke of Airdfinnan to hunt at his Scottish holding. A duke could not be denied, to the baron's thinking, and all the long ride north, Rupert and his mother were regaled by that man's ambitions for this new connection. He seemed to have forgotten that they had only been invited because Rupert and the duke's only son were friends from school. By the time they left York, his father had convinced himself that the duke had singled him out for particular favor.

Rupert had feared their two weeks in the north would be a disaster, but did want to see Alexander again. He hoped that their comrade Montgomery had been able to accept the invitation as well. The three of them would be able to run almost wild over the duke's many acres of woods and meadows. They would hunt and fish, ride and go hawking, a sport Rupert had yet to try. Perhaps there would be a country dance or two, and the food, he was convinced, would be splendid.

The house dated from medieval times and just as Alexander had oft told them, it was on an island. The road followed the river and Rupert caught glimpses of the towers rising high above the canopy of the forest ahead. There was even a pennant snapping from the tallest one, flying the duke's insignia against the sky. The walls rose sheer from the water on all sides, the keep as impregnable as Alexander had said. There was a bridge over the river to the gates, which stood open. The horses shied a little and Alexander himself walked across the bridge to grasp the bridle of the lead horse. He spoke to the beast, soothing it, and the other three followed meekly into the courtyard of the castle opposite.

"Welcome!" Alexander said with a winning smile when their footman opened the door. He bowed low over Rupert's mother's hand, enquiring after her journey. There was a bustle of activity at the doorway as a couple who could only be Alexander's parents emerged to greet their guests.

They were followed by a slender maiden with red-gold hair whose beauty struck Rupert to stone. She was younger than he and Alexander and not just lovely—there was mischief in her smile to match Alexander's own.

This had to be his sister, Miss Armstrong.

By the time she stood before him and welcomed him to Airdfinnan, Rupert was lost. Cupid's arrow found its mark in that first glimpse and throughout their visit, his feelings only grew stronger. She possessed every trait he admired. She was clever and practical, she could ride and was a better shot than he was. Her laughter filled him with delight and there was no greater triumph than prompting it. He found her on rainy afternoons in the library, curled in a great chair before the fire, and they talked about books and travel, their conversation flitting between topics as if they had known each other all their lives.

Rupert intended to wait. He planned to court her. When her family came to London for her debut season, he had made all his preparations. He would attend the masquerade and gain her attention: he did not expect to steal her heart so readily as that. A campaign had to be waged and, knowing her taste in books, a mystery might stimulate her curiosity.

But his father saw fit to bring his mistress to the duchess' masquerade ball, instead of the baroness, his wife. When Rupert arrived with his mother just as his father was being announced, the duke's frosty glance at the baron was sufficient to chill all the champagne in London, and much of it on the Continent besides. The duke had barely acknowledged the baron and did not speak to Mrs. Blythe. Instead, he bowed low over the baroness' hand and requested a dance. He had swept Rupert's delighted mother toward the dance floor as if she was the belle of the ball. The duchess had turned her back upon Rupert's father, then the entire company had ignored both him and Mrs. Blythe. Rupert had been glad to be disguised behind his mask.

His father had never forgotten what he saw as an undeserved insult.

His mother had remained a devoted friend of the duchess all her life.

And Rupert had been fool enough to argue with his father over the situation the next day, convinced as he was that he was in the right and justice must win. Oh, he had been young and in love! But as a result of that argument, Rupert was now a penniless valet, with no right to even profess his admiration for the lady who still held his heart.

Could the situation not be saved? He was the man who solved all the riddles: Haskell had to find a solution to this conundrum.

The obvious one, that he should reconcile with his father, was utterly out of the question.

Lady North Barrows was a formidable older lady with silver hair, attired entirely in black. She was stern with her granddaughters, but Anthea spied a gleam of fondness in her eyes more than once over their late luncheon. It said much for the older woman's character that she had brought the two orphaned girls into her home after the sudden deaths of their parents. To undertake the task of raising and educating them at her age spoke volumes about her commitment to them.

The sisters were polite and made good conversation over the meal, neither interrupting nor leaving an awkward silence. As was right and proper, Daphne was more actively engaged, while Miss Eurydice remained silent unless addressed directly.

The meal was marvelous as ever, but Anthea noted that her brother ate very little. She wondered at his ruse and was determined to learn the truth from him when they could converse in private. She had that opportunity sooner than expected, for the dowager requested that the girls assist her in returning to her room.

"I do apologize, Miss Armstrong, but our last journey to Cornwall has left me quite fatigued." Lady North Barrows tapped her umbrella on the floor. "It was all this hastening about in pursuit of jewel thieves, never mind a wedding and a betrothal besides. So much excitement!" She smiled at Daphne. "No doubt you wish to tell Miss Armstrong the entire tale and I can only beg you to show some restraint with the details when you do."

"Of course, *Grandmaman*."

The older lady indicated Eurydice. "And you should confirm with His Grace that it is permissable for you to read his morning newspaper in his absence." The maiden in question flushed and opened her mouth to protest, but her grandmother carried on uninterrupted. "I have no doubt he has noticed that *someone* has been reading it before him and, gentlemen, as you will learn, Eurydice, can be most particular about their newspapers. I insist you ask permission this very day and I hope the duke will not be overly indulgent."

"I should never dream of it," Alexander said gallantly, rising to his feet to escort the older woman to the door.

"Do not spoil them, sir, I beg of you, lest you undo my years of labor."

"I should not dream of that either."

The dowager laughed with unexpected lightness. "I would wager that you do, sir," she charged, then continued into the hall, her granddaughters close behind. Alexander watched them go with an indulgent smile.

"She must be relieved," Anthea said when the door was closed and they were alone together. "To have the one so well-betrothed must ease her concerns for their future."

"Indeed," he said, speaking in his usual tones and taking a seat beside hers. He leaned closer, dropping his voice in confidence. "I have promised her that Miss Eurydice need never wed, if that is her choice. She can remain in my house, as if she, too, were my sister, and if she elects to wed an impoverished man for love, I will aid them."

"You are good to them."

"I intend to be even better."

Anthea smiled. "So it *is* love."

"Can you doubt it?" He smiled. "You gave me the seed. Did you see the vine?" He rose to his feet and escorted her to the window, which looked over the small formal garden behind the house. A fountain sat in the very center of the space, silenced for the winter. Four paths divided the square space into quadrants with a precision that had always pleased Anthea.

When she might have recalled a certain evening with a masked man fetching her an ice, her attention was diverted by the enormous vine that threatened to fill the courtyard. It had been planted in the sunniest quadrant, and it engulfed both that space and half of the adjacent two. It seemed all the more vigorous since the courtyard was devoid of greenery, the planters that spilled with blooms in summer having been moved inside for the winter. Anthea stared at the large flowers of red as rich as velvet and marveled that they were real.

"I have never seen our vine in bloom. The blossoms are magnificent."

"And impossible to ignore." Alexander opened the window and Anthea caught her breath at the intoxicating scent.

There was something beguiling about that scent, something that turned one's thoughts to love and romance, to the memory of a forbidden kiss and the promise of a more romantic future. Anthea sighed and Alexander closed the window, as if to protect her from the vine's wiles. "The cold nights have not killed it?"

He shook his head. "It grows several yards a day. It will engulf that wall by Easter, I am certain."

"I wonder when its thorns will sprout."

"Perhaps when our vows are exchanged," he mused.

"It cannot know such a thing! It is a *plant*!"

Alexander shook his head. "It knew Miss Goodenham was in danger and warned me of it," he confessed with complete solemnity. "I would not be so fool as to assume I know all it can and cannot do."

Anthea frowned. "Now you are the believer while I am the skeptic."

He laughed aloud and led her back toward the settee. "It suits us well to trade roles once in a while."

"And what of this role?" She touched the lace at his cuff.

He sobered. "Haskell was not the sole one in service to the crown," he confessed in an undertone. "Though I disguised myself, the better to be underestimated. We made an effective team."

"How effective?"

"It would be vulgar to boast, but I believe we made a difference."

"And what will you do now?" Anthea feared in that moment that her brother would continue his noble duty but that doing so might imperil his new bride.

"I will shed this disguise in steady increments and return to my usual self." He winked. "Our tale is that my betrothed insists upon it and I am so besotted that I can deny her nothing."

"I thought you *were* besotted."

Alexander chuckled at the truth of it, looking untroubled. Nay, he looked smug and satisfied, like a lion after a robust meal.

"She knows?"

The pride in his smile was unmistakable. "A most perceptive young woman. She saw my truth immediately."

"How could you so hide your merit? It is no wonder it took you so long to find a bride!"

"But you will see that all ended for the best." He gave her a piercing glance. "And who better to wed than the one who sees through artifice to the hidden truth?"

"Why do I sense that you are telling me something of import?"

"Perhaps I am."

But Anthea could not imagine what he meant. She left him then to savor his own satisfaction and went to her own room, her thoughts spinning. Was there any way she might announce her presence to her mysterious stranger? She would leave her cards tomorrow at the homes of those people of her acquaintance, but she did not know who he was.

She was on the threshold of her room when the thought came to her. Of course! She would insist that Alexander host a masquerade for Daphne's debut, just as *Maman* had given one for her own debut. Her suitor would certainly hear of it, and Anthea could only hope he would attend.

Perhaps Alexander might ensure that he was

invited.

"We have to tell them," Daphne whispered to Eurydice in the room they shared. Their grandmother had retired for an afternoon nap, as was increasingly her habit.

Eurydice secured the door, then returned to her sister's side. "The confession is not ours to make." They whispered together. They had been allies together since their parents' demise, no matter how they might disagree on some matters, and always would be so.

"But Findlay means to seek his cousin, Amelia, and we know..."

Eurydice touched her fingertip to her sister's lips to silence her. She was deadly serious. "We could suggest to Miss Armstrong that we visit Mme. de Roye, as she might wish to meet our former governess."

"Then we can ask her advice in private."

Eurydice nodded. "The tale is hers to share or not. Recall that she was in peril from her former suitor and that was why she took the disguise in the first place. We must be discreet for we dare not reveal her." She winced. "I would not answer to M. de Roye for any price."

Daphne chewed her lip. "Then we cannot rush the encounter, lest it is thought urgent."

"Precisely," Eurydice agreed. "And perhaps Findlay will find his truth before we can become involved."

"But I should tell His Grace. I could not bear to have a secret between us."

Eurydice frowned, considering this. "Perhaps you might tell him in confidence. He might then suggest that Miss Armstrong call."

Daphne smiled. "Yes! He will know what is best to be done."

❧

Rupert was summoned, to his surprise, to the library by Alexander after the family had dinner. He knew that Lady North Barrows had retired, for her maid, Nelson, had been summoned, and Jenny had gone to aid the Misses Goodenham. He assumed that Miss Armstrong had also gone to her room, though Connaught had been sent to bed with her cold. Jenny or Nelson would aid the lady, no doubt.

He was astonished to find Miss Armstrong seated by the fire opposite Alexander. She wore a dress of pale gold silk which showed her coloring to advantage, and the same parure of citrine that he recalled from a long-ago evening. His throat was tight as he poured Alexander's brandy and he felt the lady's gaze upon him as he served it.

Had she guessed? Rupert could not decide whether it would be better or worse for her to have divined the truth.

He wanted to declare himself, but without any right to court her, he knew it best to remain hidden. How he hated having his heart and head at odds!

"Is Pierce ill?" she asked Alexander, which indicated to Rupert that she had no notion that they had danced together once.

Was she as haunted by that kiss as he was? There was something about the scent of that plant which drove Rupert's thoughts back to that encounter. Alexander always had a blossom in his buttonhole, for he credited the vine with his own happiness, but it seemed to taunt Rupert with possibilities that could not be pursued.

"He was instructed to leave us." Alexander shed his jacket with visible relief. Haskell moved quickly to take it, then folded it over his arm, intending to depart. The jacket had a small stain on the cuff, which was perhaps why Alexander had summoned him. He had learned that speed was best when removing a bit of oil.

"Stay, Rupert," Alexander said to his surprise.

Miss Armstrong was visibly startled that her brother used his valet's given name.

Alexander leaned back and sipped of his brandy. "As I told you earlier, Anthea, we have charted a steady progress back to my customary choices, the tale being that Miss Goodenham is influencing my taste, and it will be completed by the time we return to Airdfinnan."

"It should be completed by the time you wed." The lady spoke with conviction.

Her brother's gaze sharpened. "I have a special license, Anthea."

"And you are a peer of the realm, so a measure

of ceremony is anticipated, plus I could not bear to see you make your vows like *this*." It was clear that Miss Armstrong could not hide her distaste and Haskell bit back a smile. "Papa would roll in his grave."

"You have been considering the matter."

"Ever since I heard the news, I have thought of how the wedding should be conducted," the lady confessed. She spoke decisively and Rupert knew she would suggest a scheme of good sense. "I had thought you might host a masquerade to launch the season. *Maman* always had one when she was in town, so it would be a tribute to family tradition as well."

A masquerade. Rupert's heart stopped, then skipped.

Could he contrive to attend?

To his astonishment, he found Miss Armstrong watching him, as if she sought his reaction.

Did she know?

Was that a blessing or a curse? The conflict within Rupert grew by leaps and bounds.

"A masquerade," Alexander mused. "How irresistible. Do you not agree, Haskell?"

"A masquerade is always a most welcome diversion," he restricted himself to saying.

The lady smiled in a mysterious way, her eyes glowing as she studied him for a long moment before turning back to her brother. "Indeed, there is always something alluring about dancing with a mysterious stranger," she said, her words and her attention making Rupert's heart stop.

She did know.

What was he to do about it? Honorably he should do nothing, but....*Anthea.*

"Such a ball would introduce Miss Goodenham to society with style." She cleared her throat. "It could be held to celebrate your wedding, in a month or so."

"A month?" Alexander sounded strained.

"If not two." She spoke firmly.

Alexander rolled his eyes. "You *do* have it all planned."

"There must be time for dressmakers, Alexander. A bride must have her trousseau."

He sighed. "I suppose you are right."

"I know I am right. Am I not right, Haskell?"

"You are absolutely correct, Miss Armstrong."

"And I am outnumbered," Alexander said with a sigh. "You have free reign with expenses in that matter."

Miss Armstrong nodded, clearly having expected no less. "And there must be a measure of ceremony. There should be at least three dinners and a breakfast, to ensure she meets those she should. I have begun a list, though I will consult with Aunt Penelope and Lady North Barrows...."

"I tremble at the schemes to be wrought by the three of you."

The lady laughed. "After that, you could remain in town for the rest of the season or take Daphne abroad..."

"Airdfinnan," Alexander said with resolve. "When we leave this house, it will be for Airdfinnan. My heir will be born there, also by tradition."

Rupert knew that Alexander was unlikely to leave Scotland soon after his return. He wondered then about his own future. Could he bear to be merely a valet, at Airdfinnan, with Anthea in residence, too? He was not certain he could bear the temptation, for even now his conviction wavered and she had only been in the house a day. He certainly did not want to dishonor her at all.

Perhaps he should leave Alexander's service. The notion made the pit of his stomach drop, but Rupert recognized its merit all the same.

"I hope Miss Goodenham loves it as much as you and I do," Miss Armstrong said. "No doubt her younger sister will adore the library and be content, but…"

"But?" Alexander invited.

"Your betrothed is young," she said bluntly. "I fear she may be bored."

"I intend to keep her occupied and entertained."

"Then you should stay the season and let her enjoy it all. By the fall, she might be with child."

"It is my plan that she will be."

The lady looked exasperated by his confidence. "Not *all* details are up to you, Alexander."

The duke grinned. "But I shall do my best to influence the outcome."

"I have no doubt of that."

"How long are you delaying my nuptials, then, Anthea? Two months? Three? Perish the thought that it should be longer than that."

"You had a hasty courtship," she countered. "The wedding night will be all the sweeter for the wait."

"Will it? What say you, Rupert?"

If he was to leave Alexander's service, a longer delay in London was more to his taste. "I think three months to be certain that the lady holds your heart securely is not too much to wait when you hope to spend a lifetime together."

Alexander turned to his friend. "Do you doubt her regard?"

"I have no reason to do as much, but Miss Armstrong speaks truly: yours was a short courtship and if your intended had any guile, it would be comparatively simple to disguise true intentions for a period of weeks."

"Do you think she does?"

"No, Your Grace."

Alexander smiled approval of that.

"Exactly," Miss Armstrong agreed. "We are allies in good sense, Haskell." He felt warm at her smile of approval.

Alexander sighed. "Who can one rely upon for good advice if not one's sister and good friend?" he said. "A wedding in April it will be then, and a masquerade to celebrate it, in my customary garb." He shook a stern finger at Miss Armstrong. "Do not compel me to wait longer."

"I shall not." The lady's eyes sparkled in triumph.

"I only hope that Montgomery does not lead me to ruin in that time."

Miss Armstrong gave his padded belly a poke. "Tell me it is false."

"It is merely padding," the duke ceded.

"Ha! It would take at least two months for you to plausibly lose that weight at any rate."

"Rupert has ordered plain broth for me and dry bread. I am ravenous by noon each day!"

She laughed, a most merry sound. "It is a situation of your own making. I shall not feel sorry for you."

"You should not. It showed me the measure of my intended." Alexander glanced at Rupert. "Does the timing meet your favor?"

"Indeed, it does. I had been concerned that a more rapid weight loss might induce others to fear for your welfare." He raised his brows. "Dr. MacEwan might see fit to send you to the coast and I know Miss Goodenham would be disappointed by such tidings."

"Dr. MacEwan," Miss Armstrong said with disgust. "Does he still plague your days?"

"You do not think much of his counsel?"

"Not if he was fooled by a padded belly."

"He does not exist, my dear sister, but was merely a fiction to aid my movements around the country."

"How devious you are, Alexander," she said,

pretending to be affronted. Her sparkling eyes revealed the truth of her admiration. "I hope he has not led you astray, Haskell."

"Haskell is as steady as ever he was," Alexander said before Rupert could reply. "And a hero, as well."

"So you have told me." She regarded Rupert with a smile. "But I should never have guessed before this day that you had such a talent for artifice, Haskell."

"And is that troubling, my lady?"

"Oh no, I find it most...illuminating." Their gazes locked and held for a heady moment, one in which the world stopped for Rupert.

"And I cede to both of you," Alexander drained his glass and rose to his feet, breaking the spell. "And now, Anthea, in the name of respectability, I return to savor Montgomery's hospitality. No doubt he will be pleased to learn that I am to be his guest even longer."

"I doubt he will take offense. The earl is at ease with most matters."

"And you will see him on the morrow." Alexander let Rupert hold his coat. "Have you missed him as much as he says he misses you?"

Rupert froze at that query, especially as the lady laughed. "Oh, it is simplicity itself to miss the earl. He is such a rogue. One cannot help but be charmed."

"You could do worse, Anthea," Alexander advised. She glanced toward him, startled. "I would not stand in your way."

She was astonished to silence, which Rupert could only see as a good sign.

He could not however guarantee Montgomery's intentions, which did little to aid his sleep that night. Miss Armstrong could never be happy with such a careless scoundrel.

Never.

But in his own heart, he feared that she might. What could he do?

CHAPTER THREE

To Anthea's dismay, Haskell's suspicions proved correct.

On her first morning in London, she took her brother's footman, Clarke, with her to deliver her cards at all of her acquaintances. Although she had remained in Scotland for years, she did correspond with a number of women who had debuted in the same year as she had. Elizabeth Somerset had married a French comte, Margaret Etheridge still lived with her mother and Teresa Newson had three sons by her husband, a viscount. Anthea's mother had been friends with Lady Feathering and the Duchess of Essington, and she felt obliged to call upon them as well.

Elizabeth's butler sent Clarke back with the card. Margaret's butler sent a message that the duke was welcome, implying that Anthea was not. Teresa's butler had taken the card but Clarke's expression had been grim upon his return. Lady Feathering had told Clarke that she would call, while the duchess' butler had not even opened the door. The curtains had moved on the window above, so Anthea knew she was deliberately being refused.

It was most disappointing that all of these individuals of her acquaintance still believed her guilty—or at least that there was sufficient doubt that they did not want to associate with her. It also meant that Haskell was right: the only thing that would clear her reputation was the discovery of the stolen gem.

As much as she wished to help, Anthea could see the good sense in her remaining uninvolved. How fortunate that she had a champion in Haskell.

And that made her wonder anew whether he had been her mysterious dance partner, the one who had vowed to defend her at any price.

Was there any chance of asking him outright? Did she dare?

She wondered whether Haskell's mother might be in town. She had every justification for calling since the baroness and her own mother had been friends, and there was a chance of learning some detail about Haskell's situation. She called, only to learn from the butler that the lady remained at the country house with the baron staying at his club.

Anthea suspected that the baron actually was with his mistress, and wondered whether he still consorted with Mrs. Blythe.

She returned to the house at virtually the same moment of Alexander's arrival, once again, and her heart leapt at the sight of Haskell. He merely bowed to her then Alexander insisted he take the smaller carriage for his appointment to Mr. Cushing.

"How can you be so crestfallen on such a fine day?" her brother demanded of her when they approached the house together.

To Anthea's relief, his garb was more sedate on this day. His coat was deep blue with flourishes of pink embroidery on the cuffs; his waistcoat boasted a veritable garden of pink blooms on bright pink silk, but at least his trousers were navy and plain.

"It is as predicted," she said with a smile. "My cards were not well received."

Alexander waved this off. "Who cares for the opinions of those who are so fickle?" He didn't wait for an answer but continued with a smile. "I have a quest for you, should you choose to accept. Miss Goodenham would like to visit her former governess, who is now married. She has wished to go since our arrival here, but her grandmother insists that visiting would be too much for her at the moment."

Anthea guessed that the older lady was not very interested in visiting a former servant. "I would be delighted to escort her there. I expect Miss Eurydice would also come along."

"I expect so," Alexander agreed easily.

"I will suggest as much to Daphne at luncheon."

"That will please her. No doubt a date can be

agreed upon," Alexander mused. "I would think that the governess would be glad to see her two former pupils as well."

"What is her name?"

"It was Miss Brisbane, but now it is Mme. de Roye."

"He is French?"

"Yes." Alexander gave her a surprisingly sharp glance. "M. de Roye has a house in Cavendish Square."

Anthea blinked. "She did marry well, then."

"I understand his family were in trade, as were Miss Brisbane's. Her father owned Brisbane's Emporium. I have no idea how his family earned their wealth."

"Brisbane's Emporium! There was a place of marvels."

"There were those who say it has become less than it had been. I believe Mr. Brisbane had passed and it had a new owner. The de Royes retrieved it and Miss Goodenham believes they intend to rebuild the trade."

"They have corresponded then?"

"Yes." Alexander's eyes twinkled. "I fear Miss Goodenham may have a scheme for you to be of aid in this, Anthea."

She laughed lightly, glad of the request. "I would be delighted to offer any assistance."

"Excellent. Then we are resolved. And are all the arrangements as you would desire for dinner tonight?"

"They are. I reviewed the menu with Daphne yesterday afternoon, and she was quite intrigued by Mrs. Stewart's detailed budgets. I have asked her to compile one for the masquerade and she seemed most delighted by the challenge."

"I wagered she would be." There was no mistaking the pride and satisfaction in her brother's expression.

"You truly have found a most suitable bride, Alexander."

"And in the most unlikely of situations." He tapped a finger on her arm, those eyes sparkling. "You might take a lesson, dear sister."

"And what is that to mean?"

"Merely that love does not heed any summons. It appears when least expected and perhaps even when least convenient." He smiled at her. "But that does not mean it can be avoided."

Anthea could not have agreed more.

Mr. Timothy Cushing proved to be most helpful. Indeed, he welcomed the question of the fate of the gems with as much enthusiasm as Rupert could have hoped.

"It is a question I have pondered all these years, and a matter of some delicacy," he said when they were seated in his library. The older man was slender and spry, and he wore a large star sapphire in his cravat. "If they had been found in Nathaniel's possession, they could have been returned to their rightful owners."

"But they were not," Rupert supplied. "Not a single one of them."

The older man grimaced. "He was shrewd enough to sell them quickly, and if they were sold abroad, there is little that can be done to recover them. The crown's authority does not extend so far, regrettably."

"But there must have been some compensation to the victims."

"Of course, many had insurance and it will have been paid."

"I would wager that many would prefer to have the gems instead."

The older man's eyes twinkled. "You might be surprised. I had a visit from the son of the marchioness who had a remarkable emerald brooch stolen." Rupert strove to give no sign of his keen interest in that piece. Mr. Cushing pulled out a ledger as he spoke. "The son sold all of her jewelry after her death and I bought much of it. Some very fine pieces." He nodded in recollection. "But my point is merely that this son confessed in passing that the thief had done him a favor, in a way, as he believed the insurance was more than the gem would have fetched if he had endeavored to sell it himself. It was so strongly associated with his mother that no one else might have desired it."

The older man turned the pages of his ledger, his brow furrowed in thought. Rupert could see that the entries listed the missing gems, along with the date of their theft, a description and even a drawing, along with some additional notes.

Mr. Cushing looked up suddenly. "It is remarkable that sons are so often either the mirror of their fathers or their opposite. The marchioness and her husband, the marquess, were very fond of high society and lavish living. They were more concerned with their parties than their tenants. Their son, however, is the very opposite. He could have been a rake and a wastrel, but instead, he is determined to repair the estate and be an excellent landlord." Mr. Cushing considered Rupert. "What of you, Mr. Haskell? I have met your father, I am certain."

Rupert felt his lips thin. "My father and I do not agree on many matters."

"That is a shame. The world could do with more men prepared to risk their own welfare for a good cause, especially those who hold a large barony." He did not wait for a reply, but gestured to the book. "Here is a list of the gems I know were stolen, and my notion of where they ended up."

"Notion?"

"One hears rumors," the older man said primly. "I sketch each one, lest I forget the details."

The drawings were very detailed. Rupert read the notes on the first listing. "Paris?"

"Many of them were resold again there, I suspect," Mr. Cushing said. "As mentioned, there are fewer potential repercussions after the gem leaves England."

"Do you think Mr. Cushing journeyed there or that he had an accomplice?"

"He was disinclined to trust, as well as fond of Paris. I know he went there at least once a year, often more frequently than that."

"Despite the war?"

"There are always ways for the determined. To be sure, I thought he had a mistress there whose favors lured him back, which only shows the depth of my undeserved trust."

Rupert did not comment upon that.

"These pearls I even saw again," Mr. Cushing said, indicating one item. "There was no mistaking them, for they had a faint pink tinge and were so perfectly matched. They could never have been duplicated. The clasp had been augmented, but it was inescapably the same. The lady, who I suspect had no notion of their history, confessed that her husband had acquired them for her on the Continent. I enquired after the name of the jeweler." His lips pinched. "His reputation is not sufficient for me to use him, but others do. That was when I first suspected where some of the gems went."

"Did you make an accusation against the purchaser?"

"To what purpose? They had been modified to disguise their origins and they were never mine. It would have been my word against that of another and I am not a peer of the realm. When they have passed through many hands, it is difficult, if not impossible, to prove their trajectory. No, I made a note, in the hope that such a day as this might come."

"But you say they were never yours? I thought Mr. Cushing stole from you, when he made deliveries for you."

"Oh, his thefts were more extensive than that. He had a charm that ensured his invitation to house parties and events, and he used those opportunities to advantage, to be sure. I am ashamed that I ever employed him." Mr. Cushing winced. "Family persistence had its influence upon me, I am afraid. I admired those pearls and knew they had been stolen, no more than that." His finger moved to the next item. "This was an parure of rubies set in gold. Quite remarkable. They had almost perfect clarity and such a rich color." He sighed. "Some of my nephew's thefts, like this one, might have been commissioned."

Rupert was shocked. "Someone hired him to steal that specific set? As if they ordered a tankard of ale?"

"It is done, Mr. Haskell. Some collectors yearn to desire a piece so much that they do not care what must be done to claim it. They enjoy it in solitude." He stared down at the ledger, as if deciding how much to share, and Rupert was glad of his trust when he continued. "I saw a portrait in a library several years ago, a chamber kept most private. I was only invited there to view a necklace that the gentleman wished to sell. The painting was of an actress, quite famous at the time, wearing very little save some gems. It is impossible, of course, to be certain from a painting with its brush strokes, but I thought it might have been this parure. The gentleman noticed my scrutiny and quickly concluded our business, insisting that he had to protect the lady's modesty. Indeed, I was hastened from the premises without ever seeing the jewelry which was purportedly to be sold."

Rupert was amazed. "He must have forgotten about the portrait's details."

"I wager he appreciated other elements of that lady's charm," Mr. Cushing acknowledged then gave a delicate cough.

"What of the emerald brooch of that marchioness?"

Mr. Cushing nodded and turned the page. "I thought perhaps the duke had suggested our meeting because of that. The accusation against his sister made no sense. Their father could have bought her the crown jewels if she had desired them and the son, like his father, is known for his generosity to his family."

"And the lady's honesty is exemplary."

"Indeed." Mr. Cushing frowned at the entry. "I never saw or heard of it again." He indicated a drawing of the brooch in his ledger. "It was a large square-cut emerald, surrounded by sprays set with diamonds. Quite a distinctive piece and perhaps a bad choice for a theft as a result."

"How so?"

"It would have been readily recognized, for the marchioness to whom it belonged always wore it and she attended many parties." He frowned and sighed. "She passed so quickly after it was stolen, as if she could not bear to be seen without it. It would have been difficult to sell." He looked up. "She was already widowed, so her son came into his inheritance within the year."

Rupert could only admire that the son was so determined to do well by his father's tenants. "It might have been another commission."

"Possibly."

"May I make copies of your drawings of the missing pieces? I should like to locate as many as possible."

"Of course. I would like to have them found as well, and you may receive different replies to your inquiries than I have." The older man smiled modestly. "I have somewhat of a reputation when it comes to gems and their provenance."

"I would expect no less."

"While you are drawing, I will compile a list of jewelers and pawnbrokers who often trade in such items." Mr. Cushing nodded. "I welcome your aid in this, Mr. Haskell. It is even possible that some individuals will wish to reclaim their lost treasures."

"I am glad to be of aid, sir." Rupert set to copying the drawings, not troubling to hide that his greatest interest was in the emerald brooch formerly owned by the marchioness.

Aunt Penelope arrived for dinner in a flurry of shawls and silk, her eyes sparkling with delight. An active woman of some sixty summers and Anthea's mother's older sister, she was a widow who adored parties, gossip and society. Her very presence made any room sparkle and enlivened the most dull conversations. Anthea greeted her in the foyer, delighted to see her again, and found herself smiling at her aunt's enthusiastic greeting.

"Oh, you do look well, my dear, even more pretty than I recall. Clearly the country suits you well." She looped her arm through Anthea's and they walked together toward the dining room. "Which is why we must see you wed before you vanish from town again."

"I have few expectations, aunt," Anthea confessed. "For I am not so young as others."

"Yet there are men who appreciate a woman of good sense over a giggling girl, to be sure." Penelope rapped her fan on Anthea's shoulder and dropped her voice to whisper. "And I intend to find one for you. Indeed, my dear, I take it as a challenge. Why should Alexander be the sole one to celebrate nuptials this year?"

Anthea had no reply for that, but her aunt did not wait for one. She greeted Lady North Barrows warmly, complimenting her on her own choice of shawl, then enquired after Miss Eurydice's book.

"It is very good," that girl admitted and once again it was clear she would have preferred to retire to read. It was a different volume than she had been reading the day before. Anthea saw that the author was Walter Scott. Perhaps it was *The Lady of the Lake.* She had enjoyed that book herself.

"Then we will not linger over dessert," Aunt Penelope said, her tone conspiratorial. "The better that you might read the end."

"I have only two chapters left," Eurydice admitted and Aunt Penelope laughed.

"Perhaps we should forgo dessert," she teased, pivoting to survey Alexander as he entered the foyer. "My nephew would do well to omit that course from his meal."

Alexander, who was just arriving, gave his aunt such a look that Anthea was certain she also knew of the ruse. His garb had moved another increment toward his customary simplicity that she was cheered by the sight. Haskell was behind Alexander and she caught his eye, then nodded approval. He smiled and inclined his head slightly, and even that much of his attention left her flushing with pleasure. It was too easy to recall those lazy August days on his first visit to Airdfinnan and their many amiable conversations. The way he looked at her now made her hope that his attention had been more than good manners.

How could she contrive a moment to speak with him in private? It would be scandalous if she was caught, but Anthea did not intend to be caught—and a reputation tarnished by choice had to be preferable to the condemnation she'd endured.

"And how did this fair flower bloom in London

without my awareness?" demanded a familiar male voice.

Anthea spun to find Alexander's friend, Sebastian Montgomery, standing behind her, as bemused and impeccably dressed as ever. He had arrived when she had been talking to her aunt and she had barely noticed.

"My lord!" she exclaimed, truly glad to see him. Montgomery invariably prompted her smile. His hair was a little longer than she recalled and thus more curly, but he was just as handsome as ever. He enjoyed his own mischief so much that it was hard to hold any disregard for convention against him. "I was told you were to attend tonight but feared you might find more amusing company elsewhere and leave us disappointed."

The earl feigned horror. "Am I such a cur as this?"

"You have been on former occasions. An actress oft provides sufficient temptation, as I have been given to understand."

"True enough," he agreed ruefully, then took her elbow. He lowered his voice to a confidential whisper. "Beware, my lady, for you have entered a hive of deception and illusion."

"Not here." Anthea pretended to be shocked.

"Precisely here." He looked furtively from side to side. *"Within these very walls."*

"Should I wager that there is yet another spy in the house this night?"

"Then you know the secret tale." Montgomery

looked so disappointed that Anthea smiled. He snorted. "You would be a fool to take such a wager, for I have no time for such folly."

"Even for the good of the crown?"

"Even so. I am wretchedly consumed with my own pleasure to the exclusion of all else."

Anthea laughed as she knew she was supposed to.

He shook a warning finger at her. "And there is another reason to avoid the parson's mousetrap."

"I did not imagine you had need of a list."

"One reason suffices for me: I do not wish to wed. But there are all these ambitious mamas who would argue that is not sufficient cause. I like to have a list at the ready."

"You should have it engraved and framed."

"I might!" He indicated Alexander and Rupert with a smile. "I do believe they had rather a good time of it, though."

"Any notable successes?"

Montgomery raised his brows. "Three spies for Old Boney, a counterfeiter and a jewel thief was the tally shared with me. And countless adventures." He winked at her. "Ravishing maidens, secrets, innuendo, adventure, swordplay at night." He sighed. "I cannot imagine why anyone would surrender such a life for matrimony. Next His Grace will take up matchmaking." He rolled his eyes at the very prospect.

"And what is so amiss with matchmaking?"

"It is an old woman's amusement, to be sure."

"But is it so wrong to wish others to find happiness?"

Montgomery laughed. "If that were the goal, it would be honorable indeed. I suspect, though, that it is simply a taste for meddling, or even a compulsion to ensure unhappiness in one's fellows."

"That is unkind!" Anthea charged with a smile.

"Is it?" Montgomery led her to the dining room. "Though I would not risk the comment before your aunt, it is an affront to imagine that you should have need of a matchmaker to find a spouse."

"I am not so young as that anymore."

"Pshaw! Nor are you so plain or so witless as to be without prospects."

"Is that a proposal, sir?" She teased, knowing the reply.

Montgomery laughed so heartily that a woman who knew him less well might have been insulted. Anthea had expected no else of him and smiled at his amusement. Then he surveyed her and winked anew. "Perhaps it should be."

"My lord!" Anthea did not have to pretend to be shocked.

"I would make any woman a wretched husband and I like you too well to be so unkind." He considered her, eyes twinkling. "But you might fare better with me than most, Miss Armstrong."

"I thank you for that, sir." They smiled at each other for a moment. "And it might be a better fate than whatever my aunt has planned."

"Indeed."

Anthea took a chance and leaned closer to whisper. "And what of Haskell?"

Montgomery blinked. "You would court a valet, even if he is a hero? Miss Armstrong, I had not thought you so burdened with a romantic disposition."

"I seek the truth of it," she confessed. "*Why* is he a valet? You were all companions at school," Anthea kept her voice to a whisper, well aware that the object of her curiosity was still watching her.

"Did you not know? He has not a *sou* to his name." Montgomery raised his brows at the very notion.

Anthea frowned. "How can this be?"

Montgomery waved away this detail. "It is not my concern to tally the fortunes of my comrades, and truly, I can think of no task more tedious." Montgomery grimaced as he removed his snuffbox from his pocket. He flicked open the box with enviable style and treated himself to a pinch of snuff. "The tale, if there is one, is his to share and his alone, Miss Armstrong," he said in a surprisingly stern tone.

He clearly was not expecting any reply, which was fortunate, for Anthea did not know what to say. She had always believed Mr. Haskell to be a man of principle—indeed, she had admired him for his noble inclinations.

But if he had been her mysterious suitor that night, a lack of any future prospects could explain both his disguise and his disappearance. In a strange way, Anthea was relieved, for he might not have been deterred by the shadow cast on her reputation at all. Indeed, he had undertaken a quest to restore her good name which made him a member of the small company who believed in her innocence.

She spared a backward glance and found Mr. Haskell yet watching her, his eyes unfathomably dark. Her very flesh heated at the weight of his perusal and she yearned for something she feared she would never possess.

Abruptly, he turned away and strode down the hall toward the library. Anthea recalled herself to her responsibilities with an effort: she had guests to attend. She could dream of Haskell and her masked courtier later, when she was alone.

Alexander stood with their aunt Penelope. His waistcoat was a brilliant hue of turquoise embroidered with yellow butterflies. His shoes had been dyed to match, but still, it was an improvement upon his previous choices. She noticed that Montgomery was biting back a smile, though he was not without a fondness for elaborate waistcoats himself.

The flower in Alexander's buttonhole was from the vine and the perfume it emitted was remarkably strong. It turned Anthea's thoughts in the direction of sweet kisses, romance and happy endings.

Montgomery looked Anthea in the eye. "You see what love does to a man's wits."

She had to ask. "Do you like her?"

"I do, actually," the earl admitted, as if surprised. "There is not a shred of artifice in her, and she adores him. He will indulge her, you will see, and they will become fat and complacent together once they have a few sons."

Anthea laughed despite herself at the prospect of her brother ever becoming complacent. She gestured toward Montgomery's embroidered waistcoat, which encased his tautly muscled form. "And this is another reason to avoid marriage vows? To keep your sleek figure?"

"As good a reason as any," he agreed easily, then they turned as one at the sound of a step on the stairs. Daphne descended to the foyer, her attention as yet upon the hem of her skirt. She was a vision of loveliness, dressed in a silk dress of silvery mauve, with elaborate beading along the hem and neckline. Her fair hair was twisted up, revealing her slender neck. She was clearly excited by the dress, which had to be new and a gift from Alexander. She fairly glowed with happiness as she curtseyed before Alexander. Anthea felt that a fairy princess had descended to their company and indeed, everyone fell silent in admiration.

"She is wearing *Maman's* amethysts," Anthea whispered, admiring how well the stones favored Daphne's coloring. It was a full parure, with necklace, drop earrings, bracelet and a hair ornament that gleamed against Daphne's blond tresses.

"Is that troubling?" Montgomery murmured, his

concern unexpected.

Anthea shook her head. "No, they should be worn, and she looks well in them." She smiled at her brother's friend. "I would expect Alexander to lavish gifts upon his bride, and truly, this shows his affection most clearly. I hope their match will be a happy one."

"And you?"

"I can remain in Alexander's home and make myself of use to him and his bride."

"Do you not wish to wed?" Montgomery whispered.

"Only for love. At this point, I see no allure in compromise."

"And I salute your wisdom." Montgomery bowed slightly. "If you have need of an accomplice to evade your aunt's matchmaking schemes, I put myself at your service, Miss Armstrong."

Anthea was touched and flattered. "I thank you."

Montgomery bowed again, then offered his hand. "And now we are summoned to dinner. Shall I have the misfortune to be seated beside the bride's ferocious grandmother, do you think? She may devour me instead of the soup."

"I shall defend you, if need be, sir."

"And so already we come to rely upon each other. This season may be a most interesting one, to be sure."

"How marvelous to have such an ally," she said lightly, taking him at his word. "I cannot help but look forward to the months ahead."

Montgomery laughed, Anthea smiled, and they entered the dining room together.

She was more than aware of her aunt's considering glance but ignored it.

Of course, Montgomery made Miss Armstrong smile—and she made him laugh. Seeing the two of them together convinced Rupert that their match might be inevitable. They obviously were at ease in each other's company. They found pleasure in matching wits, to be sure, were of suitable ages for a match, and there could be no objections from their families. Indeed, they made a striking couple.

And what could Rupert do to halt the progress of that happy affair? Not a thing, not when he was consigned to remain outside of the circle of events as a servant. He could do as much service to Alexander's sister as he liked—if her reputation was restored, he still would not be able to honorably court her. His life in service was not suitable for a lady of her rank, and he would accept no charity from Alexander.

It would be wrong to interfere, and yet he did not wish to see the affair progress.

He did not wish to stay in Alexander's service and see Anthea all the time, yet he could not bear to leave and be denied even a glimpse of her. He would not reconcile with his father, who continued to flaunt Mrs. Blythe and leave his mother weeping at their country house. The situation was damnable, no matter how he looked upon it.

Rupert had scorched more than one cravat in recent weeks, just ruminating upon it.

On this night, he had a notion, though. As quixotic as it might be, he wished to give Anthea a message. He wanted her to know of his affections, but also the restraints upon him. He could not write her a note lest it be found and was uncertain he might find the opportunity to speak with her unobserved—which would be inappropriate at any rate.

Fortunately, he had a much better notion of how his aim might be achieved.

"What will your sister do when we are married?" Daphne asked when she was alone in the library with Alexander that evening. He had set aside his jacket and stoked up the fire, which she knew he did for her comfort. The rest of the family had retired, his aunt and the earl had left, the house was quiet, and they were truly alone.

It was Daphne's favorite part of her day. There was no pretense between them when they sat thus, and she had learned that she could speak to her intended about anything at all. Alexander was not a man to jump to conclusions or take offense over a comment: he was thoughtful, considerate and clever, and she realized each day how fortunate she was to be his betrothed.

She could not wait to become his wife.

He beckoned to her with a smile and she sat beside him on the settee before the fire, taking off her slippers and tucking her feet beneath her skirt. He wrapped one arm around her shoulders, pulling her against his warmth and strength, and she knew there was no finer place in the world to be.

"She will live with us, unless you would prefer otherwise. Do you not like her?"

"I adore Anthea! But she is so good and kind that I want her to be happy as well." She spared him a smile, liking how his eyes twinkled. "I want everyone to be as happy as I am."

He chuckled and pressed a kiss to her temple. "That is a wish I cannot fulfill."

"But I believe you could make a difference in this matter."

"Indeed?"

She saw that he did not understand. "You haven't noticed?"

"What haven't I noticed?"

"The way that Haskell looks at Anthea." She watched surprise light his expression, then continued. "And the way Anthea does *not* look at Haskell."

"Then you mean the affection, if there is any, is all on his side?"

"Then I mean they are quite taken with each other. She flushes when he enters the room, then is very careful to avoid glancing his way."

The duke considered this while he sipped his

brandy.

"How do they know each other?" Daphne asked.

"Years ago, Haskell came to Airdfinnan to hunt. Anthea was ten that summer and I recall that they spent considerable time together. I thought it charming that he so indulged her. She was not that interested in the hunt in those days."

Daphne sighed contentment. "And so they have known each other all this time."

"One would not have known it. When I am at Airdfinnan, they scarcely speak."

"How could they when their hearts are so full?"

He turned to look at her. "You are certain?"

Daphne nodded. "As sure as I was of your truth."

"And you think I should facilitate matters?"

"I think that if Anthea loves Haskell the way that I love you, then no other man will suit her. I think that only he can make her happy."

Alexander frowned. "But Haskell has no inheritance and no expectation of one anymore."

"Yet you are as rich as Croesus."

Alexander looked down at her. "And you know I would do anything for Anthea."

"I do, but I suspect you have not thought of this yet."

He laughed again. "No, I confess I had not." His gaze sharpened. "Rupert is proud. He will decline any financial assistance I offer him."

"Then you must think of another solution.

Anthea's happiness is at stake."

"What of Eurydice? Have you a future planned for her?"

Daphne had thought about this. "She might not wed and truly, you have ensured with your promise that she does not have to. Her desire might change, though. Could we give her a season in a few years?"

"Of course, if you wish it."

"I do."

"The better to ensure that everyone might be as happy as you," Alexander concluded, his tone teasing.

"Would the world not be a better place if everybody was happy?"

"It would indeed." They smiled at each other, the air aglow with their mutual admiration, and the fire crackled merrily in the grate. It seemed to Daphne that there was no air left in the room, that there was nothing of import in all the world save the duke. "I love you, Alexander," she whispered, as awed by that fact as when she had first realized as much.

"And I love you, my Daphne," he murmured ardently. "I shall do my best to ensure your happiness, to be sure."

"You already have, sir."

Then just as she had hoped, Alexander lowered his head and kissed her soundly.

CHAPTER FOUR

T here was a book on her nightstand.

Anthea was quite certain it had not been there before. She had not chosen it and Connaught was still abed with that wretched cold.

Romeo and Juliet.

It was hardly a favorite play of hers. Star-crossed lovers who died tragically, feuding families who had likely forgotten the origin of their dispute, and a sad ending. Anthea much preferred people and characters to use their wits.

She picked up the book and realized there was a card in it, left to mark the place. Curious, she opened the volume then caught her breath. There was a domino mask drawn on the card and on the other side. The book was from the duke's library. She moved toward the light to read the marked passage.

My bounty is as boundless as the sea,
My love as deep. The more I give to thee,
The more I have, for both are infinite.

It was a sentiment to warm her heart, save for the fate of the couple in question. She wrote the passage on the back of the card and hid the card within her papers, knowing what she had to do.

She would send a message back.

And she would not be caught doing as much.

She went to the window. Alexander's carriage was before the house, so he had lingered to speak with Daphne. Jenny would not come to Anthea until Daphne was settled for the night, at Anthea's own insistence. Eurydice was almost certainly reading in bed.

Anthea opened her door to listen. Nelson's voice carried from the dowager's room, interspersed with comments from Lady North Barrows herself. Anthea had already learned that the maid often remained late with her mistress, tending to her various demands. Pierce would be belowstairs, for the sake of discretion, and Alexander would ring when he meant to leave.

She could only hope that Haskell awaited her brother in the foyer.

She moved silently in the quiet house, smiling when she heard the great clock being wound. Trust Haskell to realize that the clock needed attention. She recalled him repairing a clock at Airdfinnan once, and her fascination at his skill with the tiny pieces. He was patient and thorough, as well as unafraid to step up when a task had to be done.

She paused on the bottom step with the book, taking a moment to watch him. He moved deftly as he finished winding the clock, adjusted the time by a minute or two, replaced the key in the case, then closed the case carefully. The clock seemed to tick more loudly as if it appreciated his efforts. She watched him take a step back and watch the clock.

She took the last step, ensuring it was audible.

He started, then pivoted and bowed. "Miss Armstrong."

"How fortunate a meeting, Mr. Haskell."

"Is it, my lady?"

"I thought you might have left already."

"His Grace wished a moment with his betrothed first."

"Are they in the library?"

"They are indeed."

"How regrettable." She lifted the book and saw his eyes light in recognition. "I fear I have the wrong book, but I would not interrupt them."

"The wrong book, my lady?"

"This one is filled with admirable sentiment but it ends badly."

"Many love affairs do end badly, my lady."

"That may be so, I prefer to believe that love conquers all obstacles. Surely the divine will must be on the side of love?"

"Oftimes, it seems otherwise."

"All the more reason to believe, then."

"And what book would you read, my lady?"

"The volume of Shakespeare's sonnets," Anthea said. "As lovely in language yet with sentiment more aligned with my own views."

"Truly?"

"Truly. I have a great affection for Sonnet 116." Anthea held his gaze and quoted.

"Let me not to the marriage of true minds
Admit impediments. Love is not love
Which alters when it alteration finds,
Or bends with the remover to remove.
O no! it is an ever-fixed mark
That looks on tempests and is never shaken..."

Haskell frowned. "But poetry is merely sentiment, my lady, and does not always acknowledge the constraints of life."

"Perhaps not, but I will speak bluntly, Mr. Haskell. I would thank you again, for endeavoring to clear my name, and also for taking on the quest of finding the missing gem." She smiled. "You guessed aright that my acquaintances are not welcoming my return to town, and I fear that it may influence Miss Goodenham's reception. I could not bear for her to pay any price on my behalf."

He immediately was concerned and she admired that he tried to reassure her. "Nor should I, but Mr. Cushing was most helpful today. He had sketches of all the missing gems, a complete inventory, I believe, and generously shared all he knew with me."

"That was most kind."

"He, too, would like to see the gems found." Haskell frowned slightly. "I wonder, my lady, if you might recount to me the details of that unfortunate incidence. It is suspected that the thief used unwitting guests to carry the stolen gems away from the site of the theft, then waylaid them, but I would like to be certain of the details."

"I am convinced that is precisely what occurred," Anthea said. "My maid Connaught had fallen ill, so we were the first to leave the house party. She has a weakness for colds and I cannot bear to see her work when she should retire to bed."

"That is most kind of you."

"It is the only decent way to treat a maid."

He smiled and her heart fluttered at the warmth in his gaze. "Yet not all do as much. Yours is a kindly nature."

Anthea found herself both pleased and agitated. "Our departure was untimely, though, for the theft of the gem was discovered immediately after we left. A party was sent after us, for a housemaid insisted she had seen the gem in Connaught's hand and I had admired it rather fulsomely. It was an emerald brooch, set with many diamonds. Quite a spectacular piece."

"But you cannot have been the only one to admire it."

She smiled and shook her head ruefully. "But I was the sole one to depart early."

"And the housemaid's tale?"

Anthea frowned. "I remember that she was one who liked to have the attention of all upon her. It could very well have been a tale told for attention. Connaught swore she never touched it, and she has served our family twenty years. She was my mother's maid before mine. In my debut year, my mother insisted that I have a fully trained lady's maid and she hired a younger girl."

"You believe Connaught."

"Of course! I told them as much when we were pursued by authorities."

"Where did they reach you?"

"We had stopped at a tavern near London for a hot meal." Anthea named the tavern and he nodded, as if he knew it. "I wished to ensure that Connaught grew no more ill and I was famished myself. Imagine my surprise when Mr. Nathaniel Cushing appeared and insisted that he buy us luncheon."

"He must have followed you."

"Indeed. And he left first, citing an appointment, but Connaught noticed that he lingered in the yard instead of hastening away. I saw later that my cases had been opened, but I suspected the boys in the yard at the tavern. I could not see that any item was missing and thought it mischief at root, then the authorities arrived with their accusations." She flushed in memory. "It was most awkward, but I granted them leave to search all of our belongings."

"And your persons?"

"No," Anthea said. "I would not endure it,

though Connaught was obliged to do as much. In the end they found nothing at all and released us, but another coach from the party had arrived and their whispered speculation was pure venom." Her old anger at the injustice of it all straightened her spine. "I have never had strangers doubt the veracity of my word and cast aspersions upon my nature with no evidence whatsoever, and I decided I would not tolerate such behavior a moment longer. We rode to Airdfinnan instead of this house, and I have been there ever since."

"I cannot blame you for such a decision," Haskell said. "Indeed, it seems most prudent given the prejudice against you. No lady of merit should have had to suffer such treatment."

She smiled at him. "And so I should have continued to suffer, without your happy efforts. I owe you more thanks than can be readily granted, Mr. Haskell."

"My lady, I merely..."

Anthea took a breath and stepped closer. Feeling most daring, she laid a hand upon his arm. Haskell froze, his gaze locked upon her. "There was a time when I dreamed we might once come to an understanding," she said quietly.

He inhaled sharply but did not move away. "I shared that hope, my lady, but now I know it to be impossible." He touched her hand fleetingly. "You should choose a suitor and wed, Miss Armstrong."

"I am not obliged to do as much..."

To her delight, his fingertip landed across her

lips. She stared at him, lost in the darkness of his eyes. He was so earnest. "But you must. You must live a full life and be happy, instead of yearning for what cannot be."

Anthea's chest was tight. "I am told your fortunes have changed."

He sighed and looked across the foyer. "By my own deed, but I would not recall it. I could not, even to please you."

"Will you confide in me?"

His smile was sad. "My situation changed after your masquerade ball." His gaze clung to hers. "You must remember my father's error."

"How could I forget it?" It was too easy to recall the unexpected arrival of Baron Thornedyke with his mistress instead of his wife—as well as Mr. Haskell's subsequent arrival with his mother. She also remembered her father's insistence upon dancing with the baroness and snubbing Mrs. Blythe. She could still see the red suffusing the baron's features and his son's impassive expression. Rupert's eyes had flashed, though, and she had admired that he was indignant on his mother's behalf.

But not truly surprised, to be sure.

"I argued with him the next day, for he was wrong to treat my mother thus." He spoke with admirable resolve. "I told him to cease his public affections with that woman, and he told me I had no right to chastise him. We argued most heatedly and in the end, he cast me out and vowed to change his will, bestowing all his possessions upon the young son he had by that woman."

Anthea was shocked. "But surely you could challenge the will."

"Perhaps I could. The stain upon our name is such that I want nothing of his. And so—" he bent and touched his lips to the back of her hand "—my own aspirations must be put aside. I will content myself with being of service to you."

"And what if I am not content with that?"

"Then you must learn to be, my lady." He bowed then, obviously intending to step away from her.

"Do you think so little of my character that you assume I will only be happy in a wealthy situation? Truly, you think love has little merit, if that is so."

He surveyed her. "I think it is easy for anyone to discount the power of money when one has it. It takes the loss of it to show the full extent of its influence."

"But..."

His grip tightened on her fingers. "I have no doubt that your heart is true, my lady, but I have watched my mother's love fade as the future she desired and expected was taken from her, one increment at a time. I would hope to never watch a woman be so disappointed again, and I certainly will not be responsible for such a situation."

Anthea did not loosen her grip upon his arm. "Will you come to the masquerade and dance with me, one last time?"

His gaze searched hers before he shook his head. "It would be unkind to both of us."

Anthea tried to tease him, just a little, hoping to prompt his smile. "Your principles, sir, begin to vex me."

"My principles, my lady, are all that I have left." His voice caught on the confession, making Anthea realize that this choice was not easy for him. "You should know that I mean to seek the gems and locate as many as possible, my lady." His gaze clung to hers even as she realized the import of his words. "We are unlikely to see each other after this night." He bent to kiss her hand again, but Anthea wanted more than that.

If this was to be their parting forever, she would have another kiss.

She reached for him and touched Haskell's jaw with her fingertips. He froze and stared at her, startled by her breach of propriety. Anthea did not care.

This time, she would choose to be scandalous, for the sake of love.

She touched her lips to his, a sweet caress that left her trembling, and hoped that he would accept her invitation. He whispered her given name, hesitated only a moment, then slanted his mouth over hers. Anthea rose to her toes, twining her fingers into his hair and demanding more.

If this was to be their last kiss, she would make it one to remember.

Anthea kissed him.

She was the most tempting woman alive and the queen of his heart, the one person most determined to undermine his principles—and the one most likely to succeed. Rupert clung to the certainty that he made the right choice, even as he reveled in her sweet kiss.

He would do anything for her, but he would not disappoint her. He would not condemn her to a life that was less than she deserved, even to have her by his side. He would protect her from anything and anyone.

Even himself.

Her kiss was a glorious temptation to forget all he knew to be true, and Rupert savored every second of it. His arm was around her waist and she pressed against him, filling his senses with her touch and the faint scent of her perfume. Her fingers were in his hair, her light caress making him burn for more than just one kiss...

A subtle cough from the direction of the library made him straighten abruptly and turn away from the alluring lady. The back of his neck heated and he could not meet Alexander's gaze. He was well aware that Miss Goodenham stood at his friend's side, though her expression was less formidable. She kissed the duke's cheek, then retreated upstairs, looking curiously satisfied.

"Alexander, I must explain..." Miss Armstrong began, but the duke pointed imperiously to the second floor.

"There is nothing to be said, Anthea."

Miss Armstrong hesitated, then retreated, her slippers tapping on the stairs until there was no sound at all.

Rupert fully expected to be chastised by his old friend and braced himself for it.

Instead, Alexander did not speak. The silence between them was oppressive to Rupert's ears and he wished Alexander would say something so that he could apologize. They left the house and got into the carriage, the air crisp and cold. They had ridden a block, alone in the carriage together, before the duke spoke. His gaze was fixed upon the window. "I would grant her an allowance," he said softly.

Rupert shook his head, even as he was awed by his friend's offer. "You have already been more than generous."

Alexander impaled him with a glance. "I would see her happy."

"I could not bear to dishonor her."

The duke sighed. "You were always the principled one."

"I am sorry. My admiration for the lady overwhelmed my duty..."

Alexander interrupted him. "You could reconcile with *him*."

"Impossible. I vowed I would do as much only if he put Mrs. Blythe aside."

The duke nodded. "I see your reasoning in that. To betray your pledge to one woman would be no guarantee that you would be reliable to another."

Rupert nodded, glad to be understood.

Alexander studied him. "You could take orders. I would find you a living."

Rupert shook his head again. "Such a life would not suit your sister well and you know it." When Alexander did not speak, he continued. "She deserves more than such a life. I would not see her raising chickens and pinching pennies, would you?"

Alexander almost smiled. "I could buy you a commission."

Rupert was surprised by his friend's generosity. "And how would I repay you?"

"By making my sister happy."

"And would she be happy, following an army?" Rupert shook his head, haunted by the memory of his own mother's disappointment. "She is a lady. She was raised to be a lady and to have such aspirations. She needs a house to manage, a garden to plan, children to teach and to spoil. She needs the security of a country house, and perhaps a townhouse in town. She needs to dance at balls and welcome guests for tea."

Alexander smiled. "You have planned quite the future for her."

"It is no jest. She is the finest of women and she should have the best that can be offered to her. I had always doubted that Thornedyke Manor would be sufficient, but less than that? The wife of a valet? It is absolutely out of the question."

Alexander looked out the window again, his expression thoughtful. "And she agrees?"

"She is romantic."

His friend nodded. "That kiss leaves me wondering whether she shares your reservations."

"She may not share them now, but it is inevitable that she will," Rupert insisted. "I will not watch affection die for lack of coin, Alexander. I have witnessed my mother's disappointment and it has torn my heart. I will not do as much to the lady I hold in highest regard."

To his relief, his friend nodded once, though his expression was solemn. "You will tell me if there is any way I can be of assistance."

"You have already been kind." Rupert sighed. "I ask your leave to seek the gems tomorrow. Some may be in France."

Alexander met his gaze, his concern clear. "It will be a dangerous quest."

"It must be done. I have no reservations."

Alexander frowned but he did not argue the matter. Which meant that in his own heart, he knew that Rupert was right. "Then Godspeed to you."

Rupert would see Miss Armstrong's name cleared, then leave the duke's household as soon as possible. The prospect of never seeing Anthea again did not fill him with joy. The possibility of her marrying Montgomery brought him even less pleasure.

The wretched truth of it was that he had no choice: he could not discard honor in the name of love and that meant Rupert would have honor alone.

He did not have to like the truth of it.

It was a fortnight after Anthea's arrival in town that a visit was arranged to the house of the de Royes in Cavendish Square. Both Daphne and Eurydice were thrilled to restore the acquaintance with their former governess, but the dowager insisted that she would forgo the visit if Anthea accompanied them. She sent her greetings and goodwill, and Anthea was happy of the outing.

"M. de Roye is most wickedly handsome," Eurydice informed her when they were in the carriage. "Theirs is a most romantic tale."

"Indeed?"

Daphne continued the tale. "He worked for her father at Brisbane's Emporium, and Miss Brisbane was utterly in love with him years ago." She sighed contentment at this detail.

Eurydice sat forward, eyes shining. "Her brother, though, gambled heavily and was in debt to a villain."

"Truly?"

"Truly," Eurydice confirmed. Anthea already saw that the younger woman loved to recount stories. "It was all the villain's scheme, for Miss Brisbane had spurned him out of her love for M. de Roye and he vowed vengeance. He seized the Emporium after her father's death, for the brother lost it in the gaming hells..." Her voice faltered and Anthea wondered whether she knew the details of the tale. It was perhaps more fitting that she did not.

"But M. de Roye vowed to retrieve it all for her and he did," Daphne concluded brightly. A quick glance was exchanged by the sisters, and Anthea wondered at it. "And then they wed."

"And now they intend to rebuild the reputation of Brisbane's Emporium," Eurydice concluded.

"You could be of assistance, Anthea," the older sister said earnestly.

Anthea smiled. "I suspect, Daphne, that you might be more so."

"I do not understand."

"You will be the toast of the *ton* this year, if my brother has anything to say of the matter. If you let it be known that you only shop at Brisbane's, then that might make a great difference in their fortunes."

The younger woman's eyes lit with excitement and then resolve. "I shall ask Mme. de Roye about it. She is a most sensible woman and will undoubtedly have a plan."

Mme. de Roye proved to be of an age with Anthea, with hair that was a little more reddish. Her eyes sparkled with good humor and she looked to be pregnant. Her affection for the Goodenham sisters could not have been feigned. Their warm exchange of greetings made Anthea smile.

The house was large and welcoming, though the fact that it was in need of some refurbishing could not be disguised.

"My husband's grandmother owned it," Mme.

de Roye confessed, glancing over the sweeping staircase. "And he spent many happy hours here both in his youth and after inheriting it. I fear he did not keep up with the repairs. We intend to refurbish it completely, but have been much involved at the emporium this winter. There is so much to be done!"

"And you must tell us every detail," Daphne urged.

The drawing room was large and comfortably furnished, filled with golden morning sunlight. They were served tea and little cakes, and Anthea simply listened as the sisters caught up on their governess' news. She was surprised that the butler was black, a most unusual situation in London. Many houses had one black servant, but they were seldom in positions of authority.

He came to the drawing room and bowed, a most handsome man with an elegant manner. "M. de Roye asked me to inform you that he will be home for dinner after all, madame," he said softly.

"How wonderful, Larousse," Mme. de Roye acknowledged. "I am glad that he was able to arrange as much. Thank you." She smiled when she apparently noted Anthea's glance. "Larousse has served my husband as valet and friend for many years," she said. "He came with him from Saint Domingue."

Larousse pivoted at the doors, inclined his head, then retreated, closing the doors behind him.

"Is that in the West Indies?" Anthea asked.

"Yes, Lucien's family grew sugar cane, which was the source of their wealth. I spent my childhood on St. Maurice, another island, so we share a love of that part of the world."

Anthea frowned, for it was curious that she had recently heard another mention of the West Indies. "I don't suppose you ever knew of a governess named Amelia Findlay?" she asked, then was startled when Mme. de Roye spilled her tea. "I ask only because our butler is seeking his cousin. He last heard of her when she took a post with a family departing for the West Indies and was hoping to find some news of her while in town. It was a number of years ago, however."

Mme. de Roye had paled. A glance passed between the other three women like quicksilver and Anthea knew there was something she did not understand.

"I apologize if my question was inappropriate," she said. "I simply hoped to be of assistance..."

Mme. de Roye set aside her tea cup and fixed Daphne with a look. "You are certain that your confidence is not misplaced?"

"I would trust Miss Armstrong with my heart and soul," Daphne replied with welcome resolve. Miss Eurydice nodded agreement.

Mme. de Roye moved to the seat beside Anthea. "I tell you this in confidence, Miss Armstrong, and hope that you do not think the less of me for it. I refused a man who then vowed to destroy all I loved. Miss Findlay was my governess and my friend, my sole ally after the death of my father and brother. And when she died, she insisted that I take her name instead, the better to hide from the villain, and lay her to rest under my name. She was quite resolute." The other woman took a shaking breath. "And so I became a governess and found a post in Cumbria with two delightful young ladies." She smiled at the Goodenham sisters. "Until we were summoned to Cornwall and Lucien—M. de Roye— unveiled my ruse and brought the fiend to justice."

This could not be all of the tale, but the details were not of Anthea's concern. "It seems that many disguises have been pierced in Cornwall of late," she contented herself with saying.

Daphne blushed crimson, but her eyes danced. "Perhaps it is the sea air," she suggested with a welcome note of mischief.

"Might I send Findlay to see you?" Anthea asked. "I am certain he would be glad to hear of his cousin's fate from you directly. His discretion is absolutely assured."

"Of course," Mme. de Roye said. "I still have her spectacles and several of her cherished books. I would be delighted to return them to her family."

That mystery solved and their course of action resolved upon, the women's conversation turned them to the season ahead and the new arrivals of fabric at Brisbane's Emporium. Daphne immediately suggested they make an appointment to view the inventory and Anthea saw the realization dawn in Mme. de Roye that the patronage of this particular duchess could remake their reputation with haste.

She sat back and sipped her tea, glad to have contributed to two most suitable resolutions.

Haskell's crossing to France was perilous and his journey to Paris more so. His French, fortunately, was excellent, and his progress proved that he could pass as a Frenchman when necessary. He found rooms in Paris in a quarter that was not entirely disreputable and began to seek out the jewelers on the list from Mr. Cushing. It promised to be a delicate business to try to find tidings of the gems without buying them outright himself and the delays chafed at him.

As the weeks passed and spring dawned upon the city, he began to wonder whether he would return to London in time for the birth of Anthea and Montgomery's first child.

The one gem of which he could discover nothing, though, was the marchioness' emerald, and he would not halt until he had located it.

For Anthea's sake.

Anthea's days in town settled into a rhythm that was not unpleasant, but certainly did not meet her aunt's expectations. She had no obligations to call on anyone and received few visitors herself. The one house where she was always received was in

Cavendish Square and she became friends with Sophia de Roye. She accompanied Daphne on her expeditions to dressmakers and glovemakers, which invariably included a visit to a bookseller for Eurydice. She discussed the finances of the household and arrangements for parties with the older sister, then books and authors with the younger. They ate *en famille* and conversation flowed as they came to know each other better. Alexander's garb made steady progress to his usual choices, even in Haskell's absence, and the date of the wedding drew ever closer. The vine continued to flourish, virtually encasing the house with its vigorous growth, and the blooms began to fade.

That did not keep Anthea's thoughts from Haskell or romance. Her aunt strove to cast eligible men into Anthea's path, making introductions at every opportunity, but not a one of them caught her interest—and truly, it was difficult to admire any man who was so swayed by rumor and innuendo. It was all too easy to recall that the men who believed in her innocence were her brother and his two friends, and that did not help her to forget Haskell. She had to believe that he would return for the wedding, and surely then, if he had fulfilled his pledge to find the gems, she might manage to change his thinking.

Montgomery was as good as his word. Whenever Anthea found herself snubbed or that people quietly turned their backs upon her, Montgomery invariably appeared. He made her smile; he flattered her shamelessly and he must have danced with her more times than he desired. Her aunt also came frequently to Anthea when they were out, to introduce one young man or another, but these potential beaux invariably melted into the crowd as soon as Aunt Penelope looked away. Alexander was also gallant in ensuring that she was not alone, but he was much engaged in escorting Daphne and introducing her.

Anthea supposed it was only natural that she began to think about retreating to Airdfinnan. The gossips had her and Montgomery making a match, which was ridiculous but a result of his gallantry. That was an unexpected side of his nature and one that explained why he, Alexander and Haskell were such good friends. She had known that Alexander and Haskell were honest and principled, and to be sure, it was a relief to realize that Montgomery, despite his talk, was similar in character.

Several weeks after their initial meeting, Anthea accompanied Daphne and Eurydice to Brisbane's Emporium. They had been invited by Mme. de Roye to view a new shipment of silks that had just arrived from Venice.

"I have asked His Grace for permission to acquire two dress lengths," Daphne confided in the carriage, then smiled. "Although I have warned him that I must choose lavish ones to ensure they attract attention. No doubt they will be expensive."

"But he knows you do as much to assist your former governess," Anthea said.

The younger woman smiled. "He insisted that I

choose two more, one for you and one for Eurydice." She beamed with pride. "He is most generous."

"He is indeed," Anthea agreed.

Daphne frowned a little. "I fear he might be too generous," she dared to say, her gaze flicking to Anthea. "I have no experience of living in a duke's home, but it seems there are many maids and footmen."

"Many," Eurydice agreed without looking up from her book.

Anthea smiled that her own view was shared. "You must have had several in Lady North Barrows' residence."

"There were the three of us, plus Nelson and Jenny, a housekeeper with a maid—it was Mrs. Jones and her daughter from the village—and always a cook with a scullery maid in the kitchens. We had neither a butler nor a footman. Seven of us lived in the house in total, and the dower house was not small."

"But there are some tasks that men do more readily," Anthea said.

"My cousin, Daniel, would send a man from the main house whenever we had need of one. Likewise, he was kind in lending us a coach and team, or inviting us to ride to hunt."

"Only Daphne liked that," Eurydice supplied.

"He let you borrow his books," Daphne countered and her sister smiled in memory.

"I cannot even think how many servants the

duke employs," she said then, turning the page of her book. It was *The Castle of Otronto*.

"Fifteen footmen, nineteen maids, two butlers, a valet, a cook, a housekeeper, a coachman, an ostler and two stableboys," Daphne said with precision. "Doubtless there are more at Airdfinnan." She looked to Anthea for confirmation.

"Only two footmen and five maids, a cook, a housekeeper, and of course, the coachman and butler who are presently here. I think there are four boys in the stables and a huntsman, as well."

"And when we return there, will all this household accompany us?"

"I am not certain of the duke's plans in that regard."

"It makes little sense to take so many footmen and maids to Scotland," Daphne said. "And even less to leave them resident here with no one to serve." She looked out the window, clearly thinking. "If we are to stay in Scotland, I wonder if we should not close up the house here. I could write letters of recommendation for those servants we release, but I do not wish to cause offense with such a proposal."

"That is a most admirable suggestion," Anthea said, seeing that some of the responsibilities of Alexander's household were leaving her grasp. "Perhaps you should discuss the possibilities with the duke."

"I think I shall, so long as you do not feel that I am intruding."

"How can you intrude? You will be duchess, and

the choices are yours to make." Anthea spoke with a smile, wanting to reassure Daphne, but she realized that her own role would be much diminished. In truth, she liked to be busy and the notion of having time on her hands was not a welcome one.

But she would not wed simply to avoid boredom, not at this point in her life. Love and love alone would suffice.

When would Haskell return?

CHAPTER FIVE

T he silks were so exquisite that it was difficult to choose. In the end, Daphne chose a length of shimmering white, lavishly embroidered with gold and silver thread and embellished with beads. It would be made into a dress for her wedding. She also chose a deep crimson with gold embroidery that suited her very well. Eurydice chose an amber silk that seemed simple but caught the light in a most attractive way. Anthea chose a silvery green at the insistence of all the others.

Then M. de Roye asked if he could have a word with her. She left the others as they chose satin slippers to match their silks, and followed him to a back room. "I would seek your advice, Miss Armstrong, if you do not mind."

"Of course not."

"I intended to give Sophia a piece of jewelry, as she desired only a simple gold band for a wedding ring. I would like to have some token to commemorate that day."

Anthea smiled. "An admirable notion."

He closed the office door behind her and an older man stood up from the chair where he had obviously been waiting. He was dressed conservatively and had a satchel in his grip along with his hat. He was a bit plump and his hair was thinning on top and turning silver at his temples. He wore gold spectacles and Anthea guessed that he was a tradesman.

"This is Mr. Forsythe," M. de Roye said. "He is a jeweler who specializes in estate pieces. I want to choose an older piece for Sophia."

"The older pieces have more character, sir," Mr. Forsythe said. At M. de Roye's gesture, he opened his bag and unfolded a small portfolio. It was lined with black velvet, and a number of pieces were fixed on the lining. They glittered and sparkled in the light, all polished to perfection.

And there it was, the gem at the root of all her troubles. Anthea stared at the emerald and diamond brooch, though she tried to hide her reaction. That brooch was from no estate. Even if its owner had died in the years since it had been stolen at that house party, surely such an item would have been included in the inventory of any will.

Was this one counterfeit?

As much as she itched to touch the gem or ask

after it, Anthea did not wish to reveal herself. Mr. Forsythe clearly did not realize the connection between the gem and herself, and she had not been introduced by name.

"I like this piece," M. de Roye said, indicating a brooch shaped like a bow. The ribbons were gold and studded with small rubies. Dangling from the knot was a large freshwater pearl. The pearl had an irregular shape, not unlike a large teardrop, and a spectacular gleam. "My grandmother had a similar one, though the bow was covered with diamonds."

"A very admirable piece, sir." Mr. Forsythe removed it and handed it to M. de Roye that he could examine it more closely.

"What do you think of it?" that man asked Anthea. His gaze was fixed on the pin in his hand.

"I think it elegant and distinctive, and also that it is something she could wear often." Anthea smiled. "It seems a waste to have a truly remarkable piece and be compelled to store it away."

"Indeed, indeed," Mr. Forsythe agreed. "Such treasures are to be enjoyed." His gaze flicked to her own necklace, a small aquamarine set in gold which matched her earrings. The set was sufficiently modest that she could wear it often and she wagered that Mr. Forsythe had valued it within a shilling.

"With your approval, then, I shall choose this one," M. de Roye said, then bowed to Anthea. "I thank you kindly for your assistance."

Anthea excused herself, leaving him to complete the transaction, her heart racing. She had to tell

Haskell of this, and wished she knew when he might return. At the very least, he should be back for Alexander's wedding, and she could only hope the gem was not sold by then.

"Secrets and schemes?" Daphne teased her upon her return.

Anthea played along, touching her fingertip to her lips. "I dare not say. Have you found slippers that match the fabric?"

"Paris?"

Alexander watched his sister brace her hands on her hips and glare at him. She was as astonished and irked as he had ever seen her.

"What possible reason has Haskell to go to Paris?"

"I told you that he meant to find the lost gems. Evidently, many of them were sold in Paris..."

"Has it eluded your attention that we are at war with France? Paris is in France, Alexander."

"I am aware of that..."

She flung out a hand. "And this is how you treat a man who is both your servant and your friend? You send him alone into a hostile area..."

"Haskell means to leave my employ."

Her eyes flashed. "Is he no longer your friend?"

"He is one of my best friends, to be sure."

"Then..."

Alexander held up a hand. "And he was determined to finish what we had started. No man could have kept him from the task he had chosen for himself, and he would accept no assistance. You should know that Haskell is proud and principled."

Anthea cast him one last furious glance, then flung herself into a chair. "Irksome man!" she said under her breath. Then she flicked a nigh lethal glance his way. "I saw it today."

Alexander could have no doubt of her meaning. He moved to sit beside her. "Truly? I could acquire it..."

She silenced him with a touch. "No, you cannot. Haskell is right. People will think that we simply surrendered it after all this time." Her voice dropped. "You must summon him home with all haste."

"But I cannot," Alexander admitted. "I cannot draw any attention to him when he is in disguise and in truth I do not know his precise location."

"But that is so perilous!"

"He insisted upon it." He sighed. "We must simply wait, Anthea."

"Surely he will return for your wedding."

"I hope as much." He kissed her hand. "Have faith, Anthea, that all will end well."

She frowned then summoned a smile. "I will try," she vowed before leaving him, but he could tell by her tone that she had doubts.

Alexander sat long in his library that night, wishing he could contrive an argument that Haskell would find persuasive.

Perhaps if his friend could not be convinced, he

would visit the baron himself.

The bride was radiant.

The Saturday in April chosen for the duke's wedding could not have been a finer day. The skies were clear and there was a light breeze as the ladies disembarked from the open carriage at the church. Daphne wore a white silk dress of a simple style, the fabric and the embroidery making it extraordinary. Her triple string of pearls had belonged to her mother, and had been given to her on the occasion of her wedding by Lady North Barrows. There were fresh lily-of-the-valley flowers twined into her golden hair and blue ribbons in her bouquet.

Her eyes danced with anticipation as her cousin, Daniel Goodenham, Baron North Barrows, led her up the steps to the church. Daniel and his wife had arrived in London in time for the wedding, a happy situation that would not have been possible if Alexander had insisted upon his plan for a quick wedding. His wife wore a lovely dress of pale pink that flattered her darker coloring very well.

At the insistence of her nephew's wife, Lady North Barrows had exchanged her usual black for a deep blue that made her look a decade younger. She had not surrendered her black umbrella, though, much less her inclination to give orders. All the same, her pride and pleasure in the happy event could not be disguised.

Eurydice wore a light yellow dress and bonnet,

and had left her book at the house. Anthea had chosen her favored blue dress, though she had indulged in a new bonnet. The horses had white plumes in their bridles and ribbons in their harnesses. The entire party looked quite festive and many people waved as the coach went by.

Anthea was convinced she would see Haskell at the church and wondered how she might consult with him privately. She was fairly bursting to tell him, not only of the gem's location but of his folly in believing that she could only wed a wealthy man.

She would convince him of the merit of love somehow.

Anthea went into the church with the dowager, followed by Eurydice and Daniel's wife. Alexander stood at the altar with Montgomery, both of them dressed elegantly and looking most handsome. A number of friends and acquaintances had come to witness the exchange of vows, but Haskell was not there.

Anthea looked twice, to no avail.

Then Daphne and Daniel stepped into the church. Alexander's eyes lit with pleasure and Daphne smiled with delight, their expressions leaving no doubt of the fullness of their hearts. Anthea felt a little ache of yearning and dared to hope that one day, she might also have such a joyous day.

What if Haskell had not returned because he could not?

What if some dire fate had befallen him, when

he had no one to come to his aid? The man was too noble, to be sure, though Anthea could not have admired him so otherwise.

And that admiration, she guessed, meant that she would never wed at all.

Rupert had failed.

There was no evading the truth of it. During his sojourn in Paris, he had located all of the missing pieces from Mr. Cushing's inventory, save one. That marchioness' emerald brooch had vanished as surely as if it had never been. He had checked every possible avenue. He had exhausted his funds, and he had no reason to linger.

He had hoped to return home in triumph, but instead he had to tell Alexander—and Anthea—that he had failed.

He would leave Alexander's service and find another post, the better that he and Anthea might forget each other.

As he packed his few belongings, Rupert found that even the promise of a glimpse of his beloved was bitter.

Indeed, she was probably betrothed to Montgomery by this time.

Preparations for the masquerade ball had filled Alexander's house with excitement, even more than the wedding and Anthea could not escape the frisson of anticipation. It had been years since her mother's last ball but the collective memory was excellent of those events. With Alexander's approval of the expense, Anthea had ensured for every possible delight. The orchestra was one of the best available, the champagne was first-rate and ordered in quantity. The silver had been polished and the house cleaned thoroughly.

There were splendid flower arrangements, though none could compare with the vine. It had filled the courtyard with its tendrils and since the wedding, the flowers had fallen and seed pods had grown. They were remarkable, like large deep red beans with a high gloss. The vines had scaled the walls to the roof and it was clear that when the greenery died back, it would armor this house similarly to its sister vine at Airdfinnan.

Rumor of the plant had traveled through the *ton*, and Anthea wondered how many would attend purely to see it. There were many ladies amongst their acquaintances who were enthusiastic about their gardens, and Anthea hired four additional footmen purely to watch over the vine and ensure no one took a cutting.

It was impossible not to consider that the vine was a mirror of Alexander's affection for his wife. Anthea was glad to see how their love grew and deepened, how her brother made Daphne laugh and how she became bolder in her teasing of him. They were besotted with each other, as they should be in Anthea's view, and her joy for her brother's happiness was occasionally tinged with disappointment that she might never know such joy.

She had high hopes for this night of nights. She felt like a queen in a new silk dress of deepest blue, embroidered with silver on the hems. Her slippers were silver and she liked how the beads in the embroidery on the dress caught the light. The dress had been an indulgence, but she was glad to have such armor when she faced society in Alexander's home.

"It is perfect," Eurydice enthused from behind her. That girl had actually emerged from both library and book-of-choice to assist Anthea with the final arrangements. She was a willing helper in ensuring her sister's debut, though she had informed Anthea that she had no care for such frippery. The season was important to Daphne, thus it was important to Eurydice: the bond between the sisters was strong, indeed.

"I thank you for your help this day," Anthea said to her with a smile. "There are always so many details to attend in the last moment."

"I believe you have thought of everything, though my experience of such events is limited." Eurydice smiled with pride. "I referred to a volume providing guidelines for conduct of young ladies, and though it is an older work, there was a chapter about balls."

"And so you know what to do?"

Eurydice solemnly counted off the lessons on her gloved fingers. "Dance, only once with each gentleman who asks. No forays into gardens or dark corners. No imbibing of champagne. I should remain near *Grandmaman* to ensure that she has no needs, and if I can be of aid to you, the duke or Daphne, I should hasten to do as much. And finally, I should retire at eleven to my chamber, for it is only with the duke's special permission that I attend at all." She wrinkled her nose at this inventory and sighed. "Worst of all, I am to avoid all known scoundrels, rogues, or men of low repute, although I should *so* like to meet a rake."

"Why is that?"

"Because I have a notion that I should wed one, and I would like to discuss the merit of the idea with someone who knows more of the pertinent details." She shook her head. "I know precious little of rakes, scoundrels and rogues. It is a real impediment to understanding society."

Anthea opened her mouth, then closed it again, uncertain what she might say to that.

"But you know Montgomery," Alexander noted, and the two women spun to find him behind them. His eyes were twinkling as if he made mischief.

"Is the earl truly a rake, or does he simply pose as one?" Eurydice demanded, which prompted Alexander's laughter. "I can't be sure when he is telling me the truth."

"Oh, you need not doubt the darkness of his reputation. Though I should warn you that his taste runs more to actresses and courtesans than maidens."

Eurydice nodded. "I should like to meet a courtesan."

"I beg your pardon?" Anthea said.

"To know what it is like. It might be quite a wondrous life."

"How so?" asked Anthea, who had always thought just the opposite.

"She might have a house, paid for by a lover, as well as clothes and jewels, a carriage or a seat at the theatre. She might go to many parties and gambling hells and never pay for any of it."

"I would not have thought you intrigued by such entertainments."

"I should like to see it all, just the once. And I should like to have enough money for all the books I can read, maybe even more than that, and time enough to compose all the tales I would like to tell."

"And how does this dovetail with wedding a rake?" Alexander asked.

"I would have no time to entertain a true husband, much less to bear children or run a household for his friends and relatives to visit. I see from this event just how much trouble it is to organize one such a party." Eurydice smiled with conviction. "But a rake does not entertain at home. He attends his mistress in her abode, so his wife might do as she would with her time. I think that would suit me well."

"It might suit you less well than you imagine, Miss Eurydice," Anthea warned. "You might be shunned in society or worse, pitied by your peers, and I would never see you endure such a plight."

"People whose friendships are swayed by reputation are not true friends," Eurydice smiled at Anthea. "I will visit you, and we shall drink tea and read books in the duke's library and be as content as may be. I think it a sensible plan, though I see that you do not agree."

Anthea was convinced that the younger woman would forget this notion by this time she was of an age to wed, so changed the subject. "Are we not a handsome party tonight?"

Eurydice wore a new white muslin with blue flowers embroidered on the hem and a wide sash of deepest blue. Her slippers were silver satin and the ribbons in her hair were both silver and blue. She was only attending with Alexander's permission, for she wished to witness the festivities. Anthea did not doubt that her brother had also ensured that her attention had somehow been drawn to the book of manners she had mentioned. Doubtless, he had left it somewhere in the library where she was likely to discover it herself, or he might have given it to Daphne, who could be relied upon to surrender all books to Eurydice.

Alexander's garb was simple and elegant, which showed him to best advantage in Anthea's view. He looked dashing indeed. On this night, he wore a yellow rose in his buttonhole and its scent did not muddle Anthea's thoughts as the red blossoms had. "I have always admired you in blue, Anthea," he said, bowing over her hand. "The shade suits you most well."

"Thank you, Alexander."

"Is that not a new dress?"

"I thought I might indulge in one. My other ball gown is a little less fashionable."

"You should have ordered more than one."

"Perhaps later in the season. I want Miss Goodenham to steal every gaze."

He smiled. "And that she will," he said, donning his black velvet mask.

A cane could be heard rapping on the stairs and Lady North Barrows, resplendent in black taffeta and jet jewelry, descended with the assistance of her granddaughter. She had mustered for this evening. There were spots of rouge upon her cheeks and her eyes were bright with excitement for her granddaughter.

Daphne herself was gloriously lovely. Anthea caught her breath at the sight of her dress: she had known at first glimpse of the fabric that it would suit her admirably. She shimmered like sunlight or a goddess stepped down to earth. The silk was of the palest hue of gold and lavishly embroidered on the hem with beads and silken flowers. It caught the light, sparkling like sunlight on water. Her hair was dressed with pearls and golden leaves and it was clear from her contented smile that marriage suited her well. Her slippers were gold and when she curtseyed before Alexander, Anthea was certain his voice had been stolen away.

His heart, she knew, had long been in this

maiden's possession.

He kissed Daphne's hand as the clock chimed nine and the doors were thrown open. The carriages had begun to arrive and their guests thronged through the doors, resplendent in their best, as Pierce announced each arrival. The orchestra began to play, the candles flickered and footmen appeared with sparkling glasses of champagne. Anthea took a breath, sensing early that the party would be a success, knowing better than to look for Haskell but unable to help herself.

At Alexander's touch on her elbow, she greeted the first of their guests. She strove to ignore the space that widened around her, though truly she wearied of those who trusted in rumor. After she had danced with Alexander and with Montgomery, she had no other partners.

She watched Daphne, who stepped more confidently into her place as duchess with each passing day. Anthea had done all that had been requested or expected of her, and was glad of her brother's happiness.

Perhaps it was time to return to Airdfinnan.

Rupert arrived late at Alexander's house and stood for a moment, astonished by the flurry of activity. He had not forgotten the masquerade ball, but he had not realized the date. If nothing else, it offered him the opportunity to leave Anthea a parting message. He slipped through the busy servant's quarters and made his way to the library. His dark coat was unremarkable, though he was glad his shirt was clean. He left a note for Alexander, not wanting to trouble him on this night, then readily found the volume he sought. He made his way up the servant's stairs undetected to leave it for Anthea.

He would leave this house for good, but could not resist the chance to look upon the merriment. He stood in the shadows of one door, admiring the decor and the music. The ballroom was filled with dancing couples, all elegantly attired and masked. Gems sparkled and ladies laughed. He spotted Alexander with his new bride, both of them apparently oblivious to any other soul in the room. Montgomery could not be missed as he laughed with a lovely woman Rupert did not know. The dowager sat with her cronies, beaming approval as she rapped her umbrella upon the floor. Miss Eurydice surveyed the dancers so intently that she might have been taking notes for some future work.

And Anthea stood alone, regal and lovely, shunned by the stain yet lingering on her name. She looked to be resigned to her fate, not seeking pity from anyone, but Rupert could not bear it.

He seized a mask from the tray of a passing servant and marched across the floor with purpose. He did not care whose path he interrupted in the dance, for his attention was fixed solely on Anthea. She seemed to sense his proximity, for she turned as he drew close and even though she was masked, her joy could not be disguised.

"Will you dance with a mysterious stranger?" he murmured and he bowed before her, just as he had asked her years before. He wanted to ensure that she had no doubt of his identity.

"Do you not mean to confess your name, sir?" she asked, proving that she also recalled that magical night.

"Then I would be neither mysterious nor a stranger, and it is my understanding that both have an allure for lovely young ladies like yourself," he said, as he had once before.

The lady's smile broadened. "I thank you, sir, for the compliment."

"Will you honor me with the next?"

The lady placed her hand with his and let him lead her to the floor. Rupert savored the surge of pleasure that she was by his side, knowing it would be the last time, then Anthea shocked him with her next words.

"I saw it," she whispered and he looked at her with astonishment.

"I could not find it. I failed..."

"Because it is *here* in London."

He turned her into the dance, his resolve complete. "Tell me," he urged, and the lady did. Indeed, he could not fault her information for being so complete in its details.

"I wager you have a plan," she confided in a whisper. "For I know you can be relied upon to defend my honor."

His heart warmed at her trust. "I do, my lady. I

most assuredly do.”

Anthea floated to her room after the ball was over, thrilled that Haskell had appeared, had danced with her and ensured he would resolve the question of the gem.

There was a book upon her nightstand, one she had not left there and she picked it up. It was from Alexander's library and like the last volume, it had a card inserted in the pages. Anthea smiled to see the mask drawn upon it, then looked at the book. It was the volume of *Sense & Sensibility* that Eurydice had been reading, and the card was near the end. It was placed alongside Edward's confession to Elinor.

"I come here with no expectations,
only to profess, now that I am at liberty to do so,
that my heart is and always will be...yours."

No expectations.

Anthea felt a shiver of dread. She left her room and went back downstairs, pleased to see that there were candles lit in the library. She found Alexander there, frowning at a letter. He glanced up at her appearance, but his frown did not fade. “From Haskell,” he said, waving the missive. “I thought I saw him tonight.”

“What does it say?”

“That he has found all the gems but one. He intends to share the details with Mr. Cushing in the hope that they can be restored to their original owners." Alexander's voice dropped low. "And as grateful as he has been for the opportunity to serve as my valet, he resigns his post." He cast the note on his desk. "He says we will not see him again, but he wishes us well."

"No!" Anthea cried.

"He is gone, Anthea," Alexander said quietly and she paced the room, fighting her tears. Her brother cleared his throat. "I am certain he believes this to be for the best."

"And he is mistaken."

Alexander moved to stand beside her and she saw the concern in his gaze "You should know that I told him I would give you an allowance," he said softly. "I promised to find him a living if he took orders." Anthea met his gaze, her own wary. "I said I would buy him a commission if he wished to join the military."

"And he declined?" Anthea exhaled. "Perhaps his regard for me is not what I imagined." Could Haskell have misled her? Anthea would never have believed it but she could think of no other explanation.

"He believes you will be unhappy without wealth." Alexander smiled when she spun to face him. "It is not bad for a man to hold my sister in such esteem that he wishes to shower her with riches."

Anthea shook her head. "I do not want riches, Alexander. I desire only love. It will be sufficient..."

"I know. I believe as much and so do you, for we have the example of our parents. Rupert believes what he has been taught by his parents' example."

Anthea winced. "And their match is unhappy. I wish I could persuade him!" She closed her eyes against the ache in her heart, hating that there was so little she could do to gain her own happiness. "I would return to Airdfinnan," she said quietly, her decision made. "It is time for me to leave town again."

"But Aunt Penelope has such plans..."

"They will never come to fruition, Alexander, for the only man I desire will not ask for my hand. I fear I will be compelled to rely upon you instead."

He smiled down at her. "You know you are welcome, but I would see you happy."

"Then convince your friend to be less proud!"

"I would have done as much if I could—but would you care as much for him then? If he surrendered his defense of his mother to gain your hand, I doubt you would admire him much at all." Alexander did not wait for a reply. "I would ask that you linger another week, Anthea, then Findlay can return with you in the smaller carriage. I expect that Daphne and I will come to Airdfinnan in August. We can ask whether Eurydice or her grandmother wish to accompany you."

"Thank you, Alexander." Anthea turned to leave the library, utterly defeated, but her brother coughed slightly. She glanced back at him.

"Were you aware, Anthea, that Thornedyke

Manor is in Northumberland? You will have to pass within forty miles of it, if you return home via York."

Anthea's heart lifted. Who better to change Rupert's thinking than his own mother? She must desire his happiness! "The baroness was a friend of *Maman's*," she said. "I tried to call on her but learned she was not in town."

"I believe she has not been in town these ten years," Alexander said. "She might welcome a visit from the daughter of a friend."

"I will write to her tomorrow." Anthea crossed the library again and kissed her brother's cheek. "I would compliment your cleverness but you might become vain."

He laughed at that. "I merely endeavor to ensure the happiness of all, as my lady wife commands."

CHAPTER SIX

I suppose I can guess why you are here." Rupert's father smirked as he sank into his favorite chair at his club. "I have no coin to give you for I have just bought Richard a curricle and a pair of feisty bays. He will be the talk of the town in no time." When this reference to his son by Mrs. Blythe elicited no reaction, he accepted a glass of port, then surveyed his son in obvious anticipation.

"I did not come to ask you for money."

"What then? To beg forgiveness? You cannot imagine how I have looked forward to this apology." He saluted Rupert with the glass, then sipped, smacking his lips. "Do begin."

"I did not come to apologize, sir."

"Why else would you come?"

"I would request a favor."

Baron Thornedyke laughed so hard that he

choked. He smacked down the glass with sufficient force that Rupert thought the stem might break, yet struggled to take a breath. The older man leaned forward and began to cough, finally wiping his eyes and resuming his original posture. He took a restorative sip of the port, his face red and his gaze filled with accusation. "Of course, you would not assist me. It would suit you well to see me dead."

"On the contrary, I do not wish for your demise, sir."

"You did not aid me."

"I did not believe you to be in genuine peril. Surely a laugh at my expense could not endanger you. It never has before."

The baron winced. "You have become more cutting, son." He sipped again and shook his head. "Why on earth would I do you a favor?"

"To be rid of me forever."

"Your timing is not all bad in this, Rupert. My solicitor has suggested all might proceed more smoothly in the event of my demise if you signed a codicil, refusing your inheritance. Do you want this favor enough to do as much?"

"I do." Rupert spoke without hesitation.

His father was visibly intrigued. "Why would you cast any chance or your inheritance away?"

"I have no desire of your legacy."

The baron snorted. "You would if you knew its size."

Rupert was skeptical. His father spent coin like water. "I thought you might prefer to have Mrs.

Blythe's son take the title."

The baron considered this. His gaze filled with the knowledge that his wife favored Rupert's word above all others. "You will be back in a year with another demand."

Rupert shook his head. "Not I. I give you my solemn word. This one favor, and you need never see me again. And you will have my signature, if that is your desire, in exchange."

"What will you do?"

"I would change my name, journey to Canada, seek my fortune and create a new life for myself."

Rupert watched his father's eyes narrow in assessment. "What would you have me do?"

Rupert smiled, for this was the easy part. "Buy a specific token for Mrs. Blythe and have her wear it everywhere."

"Why?"

"Because its disappearance has cast a shadow upon the name of an innocent lady. I would see her reputation restored, which can only be done by the rediscovery of the gem."

"Can the theft be traced to me, if I do this?"

Rupert shook his head. "It has passed through too many hands."

"Swear it."

"I do."

"I shall see you pay if you are wrong." His father's suspicious nature was consistent, if nothing else.

"I am not wrong, and the gem will please Mrs.

Blythe, I am sure."

"What matter to you if a lady's reputation is sullied?"

Rupert felt his color rise. "She deserves better."

His father laughed. "You love her! Ah, your mother's son to your marrow." He drained his glass, his decision made. "I will do this in exchange for your signature, but do not return to me when you learn your lesson. The lady will not have you if you have no inheritance, Rupert, whether you would take her to Canada or not. You merely clear her name so she can have another. That is what you should know of women."

Rupert said nothing, letting his father believe what he wished. The sole thing of import was that Anthea's name would be cleared.

❧

The Friday before Anthea's planned departure, they were invited to the theatre by Aunt Penelope. Their aunt kept a box there and Anthea suspected that lady would make one last effort to introduce her to eligible young men.

It seemed that all of London came to Drury Lane that night, perhaps because many of them intended to leave for the country soon. There was a festive air, even though the night was warm and the roads were crowded with carriages. There was a veritable crush in the corridors and Anthea for one was glad to escape into the relative comfort of the private box. Eurydice claimed a chair with an excellent view of the stage, as might have been anticipated, while Daphne and Aunt Penelope embraced. More than one lady spared Alexander an appreciative glance. No doubt there was a great deal of discussion about the good fortune of Daphne Goodenham. Lady North Barrows had declined to join them, citing a desire to retire early.

They were chatting in advance of the curtain when the whisper began. It dawned at the back of the theatre and swept through the audience like a tidal wave. It was filled with urgency, setting heads to turning and plumes to dancing. Anthea wondered what the reason could be, then she saw a man usher a woman into a large central box.

"He flaunts that woman so," Aunt Penelope murmured, taking a good look despite her disapproval. "No wonder the baroness has retreated to the country for good."

"Who are they?" Daphne asked.

"Baron Thornedyke and his mistress, Mrs. Blythe. She was an actress and said to be a courtesan before he took a house for her. They have a son— oh! There he is! He must be quite fifteen now."

Haskell's father was trim and not unattractive, obviously the source of Haskell's own good looks. His hair was silver at the temples and he was elegantly dressed—but Anthea could not approve of him treating his mistress as his wife.

Mrs. Blythe was wearing a silver dress with a daring décolletage, as well as a veritable flock of ostrich plumes in her headdress. Her gloves were long and white, and diamond bracelets sparkled on her wrists. She had dark hair and dark eyes, and was a beauty even in her forties. She surveyed the patrons, as if they were her audience and the box she occupied was the stage, then removed her wrap, fairly challenging them to look upon the magnificent gem pinned to her bodice. Given that she wore all silver and white, and that her skin was so fair, the green of the stone was as unmistakable as its size.

It was the emerald brooch that Anthea had been accused of stealing. It caught the light, the diamonds of the setting sparkling like stars, and the whisper that had seized the company changed to a gasp of admiration.

"Goodness, that looks like the marchioness' favored emerald," Aunt Penelope said, lifting her opera glasses for a better look.

Mrs. Blythe preened, clearly enjoying the attention and perhaps misunderstanding the reason for it. Baron Thornedyke smiled and bowed, waving to friends in the audience, ensuring that he and his mistress were noticed by all.

"So that is where it went," Aunt Penelope murmured, slanting a glance at Anthea. "That changes all, does it not?"

"I cannot think what you mean," Anthea said, her heart leaping.

Haskell had contrived this. She could lay the credit at the feet of no other. She was smiling as the curtain rose, but the applause did not drown out the sound of speculation. It could not be that every soul gathered there had seen the gem and understood its import, but Anthea felt that everyone discussed it. She felt the weight of a hundred gazes and knew what the chatter was that almost obliterated the sound of the actors' words.

Just as her aunt had foretold, popular opinion pivoted in Anthea's favor as quickly as it had turned against her. There was a line of eligible bachelors outside the box at intermission, though the man she wanted most to see was not there.

The baroness had replied, graciously inviting Anthea to Thornedyke Manor. She had to use that opportunity to ensure that Haskell somehow learned of her gratitude.

She yearned for the opportunity to argue her case, but feared she would never have it.

Instead, she would take a book and leave it for him as a gift.

Thornedyke was lovely in May, and the weather could not have been finer. The carriage made good time and they reached the house by mid-afternoon. Eurydice was nigh as curious as Anthea and they both surveyed the property with pleasure when they disembarked. The house was made of stone, not unlike Airdfinnan, but was surrounded by lush gardens. They could smell the flowers even from the drive and the baroness herself came to greet them.

She was tall and slender, and there was an echo of Haskell's smile in hers as she welcomed them warmly. She was a little tanned and laughed when she confessed that she spent every sunny day in the garden. "Smythe, we will have tea in the rose garden," she called and that butler bowed before disappearing. Then she urged the two younger women to look upon her flowers.

They were glorious, of such variety and vigor that Anthea could only exclaim over their perfection. She and the baroness chatted of acquaintances as they made their way to a delightful pavilion, open to the air and surrounded by roses.

They had only just sipped their tea when they heard the gallop of hoof beats. The baroness turned to look toward the house as the butler strode toward her with two letters on a salver. "An express post, my lady," he said with a regal bow.

The baroness recoiled from the document and Anthea glanced at it, noting that the sender had the surname Blythe. What audacity the mistress had in writing to the wife? She averted her gaze and sipped her tea, drawing Eurydice's attention to a particularly splendid pink rose.

"And still you have not opened the one that arrived from the solicitor this morning," the butler said, a slight bit of censure in his tone.

The baroness still did not take either.

"Good or bad news, it will not improve with the delay, *Maman*," a man teased lightly and Anthea glanced up to find Rupert himself entering the pavilion. They stared at each other for a potent moment, then the butler excused himself and the baroness performed introductions.

"Is it possible that you are already acquainted?" the baroness asked, looking between them. Anthea flushed. Rupert dropped his gaze.

"Of course," Eurydice said. "For Haskell was the duke's valet. I thought you had left for Canada," she said to him.

"My mother wished me to visit first," that man confessed.

The baroness considered Anthea and her son with a smile. "And I must admit, I delayed his departure in the hope that he might meet a lady whose company would convince him to remain."

"I gave my word, *Maman.*"

Anthea looked into the depths of her tea, uncertain how to make the situation less awkward.

Rupert took the solicitor's letter and opened it while his mother poured him a cup of tea. Evidently, he expected it to be some matter of routine, even though it had come express, for his eyes widened in shock and he sat down hard. He frowned and handed the missive to his mother. She read it quickly, then gasped and paled, leaning closer to read it once again, as if she did not believe her own eyes.

Haskell, meanwhile, frowned and lifted the other letter. He opened it and read it. His expression was so impassive that Anthea knew it concerned an issue of importance.

"We shall leave you to your mail," she said, rising to her feet.

"But I have only just tasted my tea," Eurydice protested, winning a lethal glare from Anthea for that. The younger girl got to her feet. "Yes, of course, we will," she said.

"I would ask you to remain, Miss Armstrong," Haskell said, his voice husky. "These tidings bring great change."

Anthea met his gaze in confusion, noting how dark his eyes had become. Indeed, the intensity of his attention was such that she could scarce swallow, let alone make a sound. She sank back into her chair but could not lift her cup of tea—for Rupert perched on the chair beside her, his gaze unswerving.

"My father has died," he said. "He and his son, Robert, had an accident while racing a new carriage in Hyde Park." His gaze dropped and she could not read his thoughts. "Evidently, they died immediately."

"I am so very sorry," Anthea said, impulsively touching his hand. To her surprise, he gripped her fingers for a moment before releasing her hand.

"He was not without kindness," the baroness whispered, then let her tears flow.

"You should read this missive, *Maman*." Rupert offered the second letter.

"I will not!" his mother replied with indignation. "She should not write to me..."

"But Mrs. Blythe offers an olive branch," he said softly.

His mother looked up, then took the letter and

read it, her eyes widening as she did so. There was a second document with it and she looked between them, apparently incredulous. "I would not have thought it possible," the baroness whispered.

"What did she write?" Eurydice asked with an impatience Anthea could only share.

It was Rupert who replied. "My father had me sign a document, forgoing my inheritance in favor of his son by Mrs. Blythe. Since Richard is dead, Mrs. Blythe sent the document to my mother that it might be destroyed."

"She could have done that herself," Eurydice noted.

"But she likely feared she would not be believed," Anthea said.

"Precisely." Rupert smiled warmly at her. "Which means that out of tragedy comes new hope." He dropped to his knee beside her, claiming her hand within his, and Anthea's heart raced. "Will you, Anthea Armstrong, do me the honor of becoming my wife? Thornedyke is not Airdfinnan..."

"But I would wed you, sir, not your home or your title," Anthea said with conviction. "I would be happy in a hovel with you by my side. Though I know you do not believe it, I vow to spend my life teaching you that love truly can conquer all."

He smiled then, a sight that filled her with rapture. "I believe that lesson may be learned more easily than you fear." He lifted a brow. "Will you?"

"Of course, Rupert!"

The baroness dried her tears. Eurydice watched with open curiosity, but Anthea did not care. Rupert drew her to her feet and into his arms.

"She brought you a book, though," Eurydice interjected and Anthea watched Rupert smile.

"Did she?" His eyes glowed as he looked down at her. "Which one?"

Anthea smiled. "Virgil's *Eclogues*."

Rupert chuckled. "Because of the tenth poem, which ends: *Omnia vincit amor: et nos cedamus amori.*"

"What does that mean?" Eurydice asked. "It's something about love."

Anthea translated even as she stared into Rupert's eyes. "Love conquers all; let us, too, yield to love."

"Let us indeed," he murmured in agreement, then kissed her soundly in the rose pavilion at Thornedyke Manor.

It was the first time he kissed her there, but it certainly was not the last.

A MOST INCONVENIENT EARL
The Brides of North Barrows #4

Eurydice Goodenham is convinced that a marriage of convenience with the notorious Sebastian Montgomery, Earl of Rockmorton, would be ideal: in exchange for one child, she can retreat to the library of his country house to write, while he continues his scandalous life in London. But when she finds herself falling in love with her unpredictable, mischievous and secretly honorable husband, does she have any hope of claiming his heart?

Sebastian is bored with the world's amusements, until his friend's ward makes a startling proposal. He can't help but challenge Eurydice's expectations in return. A wild escape to Gretna Green convinces him that his unexpected bride is perfect for him—except that Eurydice doesn't believe in love. Can Sebastian win this bluestocking's reluctant heart in time to save a Christmas—and a marriage—going awry?

Available March 2022

Download a free family tree for the *Brides of North Barrows* at Claire's website:

https://delacroix.net/north-barrows/

ABOUT THE AUTHOR

Deborah Cooke sold her first book in 1992, a medieval romance called **Romance of the Rose** published under her pseudonym Claire Delacroix. Since then, she has published over fifty novels in a wide variety of sub-genres, including historical romance, contemporary romance, and paranormal romance. She has published under the names Claire Delacroix, Claire Cross and Deborah Cooke. **The Beauty**, part of her successful Bride Quest series of historical romances, was her first title to land on the *New York Times* List of Bestselling Books. Her books routinely appear on other bestseller lists and have won numerous awards. In 2009, she was the writer-in-residence at the Toronto Public Library, the first time the library has hosted a residency focused on the romance genre. In 2012, she was honored to receive the Romance Writers of America's Mentor of the Year Award.

Currently, she writes historical romances as Claire Delacroix. She also writes paranormal romances and contemporary romances under the name Deborah Cooke. Deborah lives in Canada with her husband and family, as well as far too many unfinished knitting projects.

To learn more about her books, visit her websites:

http://delacroix.net

http://deborahcooke.com

A Baron for All Seasons